I0556697

The Curse of the Lost Galleon

The Curse of the Lost Galleon

Stephen Kappotis

Cape Ann Press
North Andover, Massachusetts

The Third Voyage of Sloth and Good Boy
Cape Ann Press
North Andover, MA, USA

Paperback: ISBN 979-8-9859352-4-0
Ebook: ISBN 979-8-9859352-6-4

Library of Congress Control Number: 2025907787
10 9 8 7 6 5 4 3 2 1

For Dr. Rebecca Cliffe and the Sloth Conservation Foundation for all their efforts in researching, understanding, and helping sloths.

<u>Pirates</u>

By the time they saw the ship, it would have been too late to put up much of a fight. Sure, maybe one or two largely symbolic cannon shots had been fired, but it's likely that the only ones who could have survived the attack by pirate captain Louis LeFleur's sloop, *Frères de la Liberté*, were up on the same cliff Rondo Julius is looking down from today.

Already largely abandoned by 1702 when a storm drove the Spanish treasure galleon, *Santa Teresa de Avila*, into the rocks of the harbor below, the walls of the crescent shaped fort would have been little help in defense, good only to slow the enemy's pursuit of the remaining guard and survivors. If the walls of the fort's northern flank had not collapsed upon much of the remains of the shipwreck, perhaps the salvage crews could have finished their job to satisfaction and left before LeFleur's arrival.

Modern day pirates are down there now, Rondo thinks. But they're working for him. Or so he keeps trying to believe. He won't be able to convince himself much longer, as the final secret to the treasure's location will be found out soon and they won't need him anymore. If they decide to double cross him for a larger share, his only chance is the SOS he's sent out to an ex-girlfriend who certainly doesn't miss him.

However, if these pirates decide to honor their deal for shares in the recovered loot, he hopes she doesn't figure out his clues and go to the authorities before they can complete the job. After all, trying to avoid their attention is the point of working with these criminals. To avoid the government of a country that didn't even exist back then claiming the treasure as cultural property, Rondo needs the help of these shady people to steal what he's rightfully found after it had been lost by those who stole it from the original owners hundreds of years earlier.

Cultural property? The culture it was stolen from was all but wiped out! And he's supposed to believe the descendants of their killers and those who moved in later have more of a right to it than him because they inherited the geography? While Rondo doesn't dispute that there is certainly historic value to the citizens of the country that claims this territory, if the choice is between taking a risk and getting rich or turning it over and having his name as an asterisked footnote on a kiosk in a museum to be ignored by indifferent tourists, he'll go with the money. If that makes him a bad archaeologist, who cares? There's plenty else he can find to do if he can live to see the money. Besides, it was the very legend of this lost treasure that got him interested in archaeology in the first place.

```
            /\      /\                                    ~  \    /  ~
          \ 0      0 /                                      (        )
--------    \  /  \  /    ------|||---/o) _ (o\---|||------  (        )   -----
             \/                                               \ /
```

      It's almost Good Boy and Calypso's favorite time of the day—*World Animal Showcase* is on the television. Good Boy, the black and tan German shepherd, lays in front of the couch in the small house of Shriya the paleontologist, while Calypso the predominantly brown Bradypus sloth, hangs from a rope suspended horizontally along the ceiling. The rope leads to a small door in the exterior wall with a latch on each side that she can open to climb out and up to the trees next to the property or back inside whenever she feels like it.

      Shriya is on a paleontological dig, but her goatherder friend Miguel is keeping an eye on the house and taking care of the animals for her. Miguel is around forty years old, of short muscular stature, with skin a bit weather worn from a mostly outdoor lifestyle. He uses a clothespin to attach a sprig of leaves and a hibiscus flower to the rope for Calypso to eat while she watches the show. Good Boy gets up and rushes to the screened back door, barking for Juan Manuel to join them. Juan Manuel is a large Spanish goat, tan with a black dorsal stripe. Shriya named him Charleston after Charleston Chew candy because she didn't know his original name and, since he's a goat, he's unable to tell her. He looks up from the scrub brush he's eating in the yard by the dock on the river where a 5.5m Speedwell Atalanta speedboat, is tied up.

"They have the bears that eat fish on there?" he asks.

"I don't know, you know there's always something different." Good Boy impatiently turns in a circle to get him to come inside.

"I don't want to see giant lizards eating goats again."

"OK. I don't know what might show up, though."

"Or chimpanzees."

"Yup. Still don't know what might show up. Are you coming or what?"

"Yeah, OK." He finishes chewing and walks to the house, opening the door latch with his mouth, and going inside.

The show is about elephants and the friends are surprised to see that there's another animal as big as a giant ground sloth, and that its nose is also an arm. Juan Manuel thinks he could easily make friends with such an animal. They all cheer when an elephant shakes a tree to bring down the fruit and some monkeys also fall out, chattering in annoyance.

When the animal show ends, Miguel changes to an action movie. It starts with a nervous looking man driving a car at high speed down a long stretch of road cutting through a forest. The trees go by too fast for Calypso to identify, which makes her slightly frustrated because they look like nice trees and the driver is just zooming by like they don't even matter. As the man races down the road, the viewer's angle cuts to behind the car, rising above it to reveal two more cars ahead, parked nose-to-nose blocking the road. Men stand behind them with guns aimed at the speeding car.

The view returns to inside the car with the first man. The roadblock gets closer, very fast. The man yells at the roadblock, which doesn't scare it away, then he reaches down near his feet and does something Calypso doesn't understand. He pushes open

3

the door, and rolls out of the car, coming to a stop on the grass alongside the road as the car continues into the roadblock and everything explodes into fire.

The man stands up, brushes some dirt off of himself, and jogs into the forest. That's ridiculous, Calypso thinks, there's no way he wouldn't be hurt after jumping out of that car going so fast. She's had enough of this magic window for now, so she heads back along the rope to the trees outside. The spring-hinged door closes behind her and, as she climbs for the trees, she wonders if she could learn how to drive a car like she learned how to drive the boat. She's watched people drive cars, but she's not sure how to make them work other than that the wheel makes it change directions.

Good Boy's ears rotate toward the front of the house at the sound of human voices stopping at the gate a few steps from the front doorway. The gate hinges creak open, prompting him to run to the front door. Two sets of footsteps approach the porch. He barks a warning, but they don't slow down. Good Boy backs up from the door and gets ready to jump them. Juan Manuel notices and stands behind to back him up.

The people knock strongly on the wood alongside the screen door. Miguel walks to the door to see what the fuss is about, cutting off Good Boy's line of attack—stupid person! Even dumber, he just goes and opens the front door! What is wrong with this idiot? Good Boy steps beside Miguel and barks at the men, both of whom are bigger and stronger than Miguel. The guy at the door has a light-coat of skin and an easy, fake smile sitting over a squared chin. A darker-coated man in back stands casually, but Good Boy picks up on the tautness in him that's like a snake waiting for the slightest wrong movement of its prey to strike. Trained as an attack dog not to warn an enemy before engaging in a fight, he stays quiet while his eyes could start fires.

"How are you doing?" Fake Smile asks.

"I'm OK, can I help you?" Miguel asks with a little wariness.

4

"We're looking for Shriya."

"She didn't mention anything to me about meeting with anyone before she left."

"Oh, she's not here? That's no good. Do you know when she'll be back?"

"Be a few days, I imagine."

"A few days?" Fake Smile turns to Snake Man, then back to Miguel. "That's too bad. Do you know if she got the package I sent?"

"No idea."

"Maybe you've seen it? Rather small, I believe."

"You *believe*?" Good Boy heard that too, and he's glad Miguel picked up on it.

"I can't remember what I packed it in. It's a book I found that I thought she might like. I left some papers in there by mistake and now I need them." His laugh is as fake as his smile. "I looked all over, but I can't find them anywhere. The last time I saw them was before I sent out the package."

Snake Man looks through a barred front window at the small table by the door. A bunch of assorted papers and such lay on it.

Miguel's eyes follow him, but he stays cool. "I don't know. What's your name? I'll keep a look out for any packages with your name on them."

Fake Smile looks at Snake Man, who nods. Fake Smile pauses, then says, "Rondo Julius."

"OK, *Rondo*. You'll have to come back when she's home."

Fake Smile's expression becomes less convincing and he puts his hand on the outside screen door latch.

Miguel goes to grab his side of the latch, but the man is too quick and he pulls the door open. Good Boy barks and would jump, but Miguel and the angle of the door block his way. Before he can maneuver around, Snake Man pulls out a gun and points it at Miguel. Hit with fear, Good Boy barks viciously, but the two men push themselves in. Snake Man points his gun at Good Boy, spitting fury, but Miguel holds him back by the collar.

Unable to make a charge against the intruders with Miguel and Good Boy taking up the space he needs, Juan Manuel backs into the kitchen and waits for an opening, or a chance to retreat out the back door.

"What do you want?" Miguel asks threateningly.

"My package!"

"I know what Rondo looks like."

"Yeah?" Fake Smile sneers. "How well do you know him?"

"Well enough not to like him."

"He knows him, all right," Snake Man laughs.

"Then you don't need to be in our way," Fake Smile says. "This only concerns him."

"Hey, look at that," Snake Man says, pointing to Juan Manuel. "He's trying to look tough in front of his girlfriend!"

"Maybe that's Shriya and everything we heard about her is wrong!" Fake Smile says, hitting Snake Man on the arm.

"Rondo's annoying, he's not a freak," Snake Man says, ignoring the joke.

Juan Manuel makes a fart noise at him with his lips and, as he expects, the man laughs and ignores him, so he turns to the back door, opens it, and goes outside. He'll wait to ambush them out front when they leave.

Fake Smile finds the plain box package in the pile of mail on the messy table, pulls out a knife much larger than it needs to be for this particular task, and cuts it open. He smiles and takes out a journal. He keeps his eyes on Miguel, pulls a phone out of his pocket, and lifts it to his mouth. He doesn't press anything, just says, "We've got it," and puts it away. Almost immediately, Good Boy hears a boat pull up to the dock on the river out back.

"What do we do with him?" Snake Man asks.

Fake Smile stares at Miguel with eyes that look through him. "He doesn't know anything. He's not worth the heat. Let's go."

The men push by into the kitchen.

"If you touch Shriya, I will kill all of you," Miguel threatens hollowly, still standing in place in the living room.

"We only came for our book. Be smart and forget all about this and none of us will see each other again." Fake Smile grins, still staring holes through Miguel before following Snake Man out the back door. Miguel runs through the kitchen to see the two men jog to a waiting center console boat with two more men aboard.

Juan Manuel turns around the back corner of the house and charges for the dock. One of the men on the boat raises a rifle, takes aim, and fires. Juan Manuel's head jerks back and he drops to the lawn with a flopping skid. Good Boy smashes through the bottom of the screened back door, shattering its frame as the screen tries in vain to hold itself together. The boat pulls away and turns down river toward the ocean. Good Boy leaps the back stairs in one go, charges down the yard like a horse, clearing the end of the dock and making a flying leap for them, but the boat accelerates quickly away, leaving him to swim back in defeat. The current pushes him downstream so that he lands on the river bank and has to crunch through the brush to get back to Shriya's yard.

Good Boy finds Miguel sitting in the yard next to an open first aid box holding Juan Manuel's head in his lap and he rushes over to them. Juan Manuel's head is covered in blood with half his left horn missing. Miguel wraps the broken end, under his chin, then back around.

"I think I'm OK," Juan Manuel says to Good Boy.

"They hit your horn. About half of it is missing."

"I had no idea," Juan Manuel says, softly. "I guess that explains all the pain and bleeding."

Good Boy frowns. "At least your bad sense of humor isn't stored in your horns."

"It is, they just got the wrong one."

"How bad does it hurt?"

"Not as much as losing my herd in a flashflood, but it's up there."

Finished wrapping him up, Miguel pats Juan Manuel on the side and runs into the house.

"Where's he going?" Juan Manuel asks Good Boy.

"How would I know?"

"How do I look?"

"Lopsided."

"There goes my pretty face, there goes the does!"

"Nah, you've got a great story to tell and great stories beat a pretty face."

Juan Manuel looks doubtful. "Yeah, well, at least it should grow back."

"Horns grow back?"

"I think so. They're made out of the same kind of thing as hooves or claws, right?"

"Sure," Good Boy tries to say cheerfully. "Either way, it's better than a hole in the head."

"So's being covered in monkey poop, but I'd still complain."

"Do you think Calypso saw that?"

"I don't know. I think she's in the tree. Must have heard it, though." Juan Manuel gets to his feet and the friends look to the top of the tree that's connected to the house by the rope. Calypso is on the lawn, crawling in their direction.

"They headed for the big water," she calls. "Bring me to the boat!"

Good Boy and Juan Manuel run to her and Juan Manuel hoists Calypso onto Good Boy's back. They race to the Speedwell, unlatch the aircraft-style canopy, and slide it back, then Calypso and Juan Manuel load into the boat while Good Boy unties the bow line. Miguel yells, "Oh, come on, not again!" as he runs for the dock with a rifle over his shoulder, a pack on his back, and a large duffel bag in one hand. Good Boy hops inside and gets in the open back behind the front bench seat, Miguel tosses the stuff on the seat next to Calypso, and unties the remaining lines as she lowers the motor and starts it. Miguel gets in, pushes the bags under the dashboard, and sits down. Calypso looks up at him.

"You're going to leave without me again?" he says to her. "I brought food! Let's get them!"

Calypso turns her head around backwards and reverses the boat into the river. The boat rolls to a stop in the current, the lower unit clunks into forward gear, and they race down the river towards the Caribbean Sea.

Miguel stands bracing himself on the windshield frame against the boat chopping over the waves, scanning the horizon and wondering if he should have taken over driving since Calypso seems to only be able to run the boat at three-quarter throttle. He smacks the top of the windshield in frustration. The other boat is nowhere to be seen. Looking down at Calypso, the determined look on her face as she continues her fruitless pursuit of people who shot her goat friend makes Miguel smile and shake his head in amazement.

Calypso cuts back on the throttle and stares up at him and he wonders if she didn't just realize the same thing: they've lost them. He shakes his head and sits down in annoyance. Calypso continues to stare at him.

"They're long gone. We might as well head back," he says. She doesn't seem to understand, so he points back in the direction of their home. She blinks slowly then climbs over the back of the seat and onto Juan Manuel's neck, leaving the boat still going at speed. Miguel grabs the steering and trim control stick and throttle quickly, slowing the boat as it crashes down and rolls violently off a larger wave, nearly chucking Good Boy and Juan Manuel into the fixed rear canopy. He checks to make sure nobody flew out and heads back to Shriya's house.

Calypso gently taps the base of Juan Manuel's broken horn. "Does it hurt?"

"Yeah, especially when you touch it!"

"Sorry. Does it grow back like claws?"

"I hope so, but it worries me that it hurts so much."

Calypso scratches the blood-caked fur around Juan Manuel's ears the way he likes.

"How did you get on the ground so fast?" he asks her.

"Dropped."

"You mean, you fell?"

"Yes," she nods, "but intentionally."

"You're not hurt?"

"No."

Juan Manuel thinks for a moment. "You could have been."

Calypso keeps scratching. "Yes. Didn't. *You* got hurt, though."

"That was dumb," he says, "but I was angry."

"So was I."

"Anger makes you dumb."

"Sometimes," Calypso says. "Sometimes it makes you brave."

"I wish I could tell which one it is before I've done something."

She hugs her arms around his neck until they get back to Shriya's house.

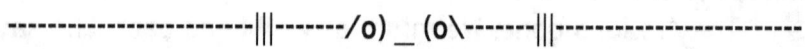

An outboard motor hums up to the dock and goes silent. Good Boy, recognizing the sound, runs to the patched up back door and barks to Shriya, who waves as she ties the Zodiac to the dock behind the Speedwell and grabs a large pack out of the boat. Good Boy opens the door with his teeth and runs to her and she stops to hug him and scratch his ears.

"There's Buca! Oh, it's so good to see you! Where is everyone else, huh?" Shriya stands with a groan and Good Boy trots alongside her to the house. She notices that the screen and some of its frame has been replaced and, when she opens it, the hinges pull out loose from the jamb and she has to set it in the latch just right for it to stay shut. With a sigh, she shuts the main door and hears the screen door fall back out of the latch.

"What happened to the door?" she asks no one in particular, shaking her head with impatience. She calls for Miguel, but there's no answer. Good, she thinks, for not having to exchange any kind of pleasantries before being able to get into the shower. The pack gets left on the floor with a careless thump and her clothes peel off as she heads for the bathroom, only stopping to check the rope for Calypso, who isn't there. The mirror Shriya gets her attention, the appearance making her wince. Getting up close, she inspects a slightly inflamed bug bite on the side of her straight nose. Of all the places! It could only be more obvious if it was at the end of her nose. A darker, spotted band across the tanned skin of her shallow forehead from where her hat brim sits looks like a rash. To her relief, she rubs it, and it comes off. There's a double bruise on her left collarbone. At least it isn't sore. Some wrinkles are starting on her face, accentuated by sweat and dirt, making her look older than she is. With a frown, she reminds herself that people usually think she's about ten years younger than her age of forty-four when she's not filthy. Tick tock goes the clock, she sighs. Time to wash off the last million years.

Shriya lays in bed wearing old shorts and a baggy Duran Duran tee shirt old enough to have been found on a dig, looking up at the spinning ceiling fan through half-closed eyes. The shorts feel a little looser than they had, telling her she's lost weight she didn't need to lose. Probably half of that was blood loss from all the parasites! At least she still has hips enough to hold up her pants. What she really needs is something to eat, but she's too tired to get back up after a week of digging at a Glyptodon fossil site in a mosquito vortex within the world's sweatiest butt crack—after all, the area just north was known as the Mosquito Coast—and wondering if she should be digging mammoths out of the melting Siberian tundra instead. No, they have clouds of mosquitoes there, too. Maybe she could take a cushy, if boring, cataloging job indoors. Quite a lot of recent major discoveries have been people taking a fresh look at old specimens. She sighs, unable to even convince herself with that argument. Good Boy sits by her side against the bed while she absently scratches his head and listens to the rhythm of the fan wobbling slightly with imbalanced blades. Good Boy raises his head suddenly.

"Shriya!"

Miguel's call jolts her to full consciousness. He calls for her again from downstairs.

"Upstairs!" she answers. "Could you bring me some water?"

A minute later, he walks into the bedroom holding a glass of water in one hand and her dirty clothes in the other. She drags herself up to take the glass and he drops the dirty clothes into a hamper next to the door.

He nods to the bug bites around the bottom of her legs. "They got you pretty good, huh?"

Shriya downs the glass of water in one go and takes a breath. "Oh yeah, I ran out of socks a few days ago and the bug spray got washed off my ankles. One of the wankers even got my nose."

"So you are saying that you had fun?"

"I think I'm getting burnt out on field work, but I also don't want to be working inside on some dusty museum collection. Maybe I just need to switch to someplace colder."

"Isn't it hot and humid in India?" Miguel asks, sitting next to Shriya on the bed. Good Boy grumbles and stands to put his head on her leg. "I would think you'd be used to the climate."

"It depends on which part of India you're talking about, but we moved to the UK when I was three and we later moved to the northeast United States. At this point, I'm about as Indian as John Smith. I should be used to the climate because I've been here for six years." She shakes her head. "No, seven years. Wow."

"I've never lived anywhere else. Do you miss it?"
"What?"
"I don't know, the US or the UK?"

12

"Some things, but I like it here. Well, I do when I'm not living in a mosquito nest." She goes to scratch her legs, but stops herself. "Sailing. I miss sailing. When I was a girl, my dad had me take sailing lessons. I still remember my first boat: a Wayfarer Mark I in GRP that I named *Magical Mystery Tour*, but I spelled *mystery* like a name—*Miss Terry.*" She shrugs and looks at the overflowing hamper.

"I was going through a Beatles phase. I spent most of my summers in that dinghy until we moved to the States and I got caught up in school and all that. I haven't sailed more than a few times since."

"Why don't you get a sailboat?" Miguel asks.

"The rigid inflatable fits my needs better."

"I mean, *in addition* to it," Miguel says. "Sell the speedboat."

"That's Calypso's!" Shriya says. "I can't sell that."

"She seems quite happy with her trees and rope."

"Still . . . it wouldn't feel right. Especially where it was practically gifted to me by the original owner's sister."

Miguel chuckles and takes her hand. "I never took you for being sentimental."

"About some things, but that's simply not my boat to sell."

"It's yours by law. I'm not sure Calypso understands the idea of owning things."

"Maybe not," Shriya says, taking her hand from his to pick up the water so she can scratch behind the ears of an insistent Good Boy, "but I do, and I don't care about what the law says, it's her boat." There is a moment of silence as Miguel drops his argument. He knows when Shriya has dug in.

"Calypso's in the tree?" she asks him.

"She's not inside."

"Where's Charleston? He wasn't here when I got back."

"He's in the yard," Miguel says. "I took him to the store with me to get some dowels and glue to fix the door jamb where the hinges tore out."

13

"Yeah, I saw the door," Shriya nods. "Can you just use some bigger screws? I should have some in the drawers above my tool cabinet."

"No, it got tore out pretty bad," Miguel says. "I have to drill out the holes and fill them with twelve millimeter dowels."

"Twelve millimeters!"

"It doesn't need to be that big, I just want to make sure it holds and there wasn't a big selection of dowels. Must be a lot of people having door problems lately."

"So, what happened to it?"

"I'll tell you later," Miguel says, rising from the bed. "Everything's fine, but you look tired."

She points at him and nods, swallowing some water. "I *am* tired. Very astute!"

He laughs. "You must be to wear such faded and torn shirt and shorts," Miguel teases her.

Shriya grins at him. "They're comfortable and—more importantly—they were *clean*."

"Well, you look good, anyway," Miguel smiles back at her. "Do you want me to leave you alone to slee—"

"What if we just lie here quietly?" Shriya says, patting the bed to encourage him to sit back down.

"I was going to fix the door. I wanted to get it fixed before you got back."

"Too late. Thank you, but leave it for now. I'll buy you dinner when I have the energy to get up again sometime next month."

"OK," he nods, taking off his shoes and lying next to her. Good Boy sniffs at the shoes.

"Now I think I know what Calypso must feel like a lot of the time."

"She loves the heat, though," Miguel says.

Shriya turns and smiles at him.

Good Boy snorts and gets up, giving Miguel the eyes of disapproval before leaving to find Juan Manuel.

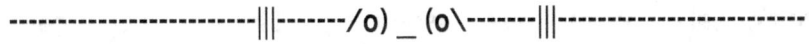

"Have you seen this?" Shriya calls to Miguel from her computer at the kitchen table.

"Have I seen what?" He asks, testing the screen door on its repaired hinges.

"This video of Pablo with Calypso. Pablo's sister sent it to me."

Miguel comes over. "Door is good."

"Thank you." She kisses him and starts the video, which begins with a shot of an empty chair. A man in his 20s with a buzz cut poorly covering tattoos that run down to his neck sits in the chair, holding a baby sloth, which he turns to the camera. Obviously excited, he is still able to keep his voice low.

"Here she is, Elaina! She's a three-toe sloth, a Bradypus variegatus—took me a while to remember that one! I bet when I told you I had an animal surprise you thought I was going to show you a dog or something, right? Nah. Yo, I named her Calypso."

A tiny Calypso clings to a stuffed bear and drinks milk through a long nipple on a bottle Pablo holds above her.

"She eats leaves, but I still give her goat milk for a little while. Isn't she adorable? I tried to give her to the animal rescue so they could take care of her, but she would only eat from me and I think they didn't think she was going to make it, so they told me how to take care of her and recommended I take her home and keep her warm, but she's a fighter, I can tell."

Baby Calypso reaches out for the camera and looks at it curiously.

"Freddy Kreuger claws! Don't mess with this!" Pablo laughs quietly. "People say sloths are dumb, but she's so smart and curious, she checks out everything!"

Calypso taps the lens with her claw.

15

"I mean, right? How can I not do everything I can for this little animal? Yo, you know I seen people I know back home shot dead and it's just like, yeah, that sucks, but now, with her little face, I can't even think about anything bad happening to her—it makes me sick to my stomach. You know people? Maybe we deserve it, but this helpless, harmless, sweet little thing? Nah, that's too cruel! The world's too cruel, yo. This is sad how I got her—dogs killed her moms."

Pablo nods and says something soothing to Calypso in a soft voice.

"Nobody cares about no damn leash laws down here, or maybe they strays or something. Her moms curled up around her to save her and sacrificed herself, you believe that? We ain't so special when peaceful animals like this can be heroic, too. If she makes it—pray to God—I'm going to get a dog, like a *big* dog, but if it don't love this little sloth, Imma trade it in for a different one." Pablo I laughs.

"No, but I mean, you know I gotta do some things down here to make bank and I could use a mean-ass dog to help protect me . . . and little Calypso."

Calypso waves, trying to reach the camera, which is just out of reach.

"Ooh, look at that, sis—she's wavin' at you!" Pablo shakes his head and the camera jiggles a little with him.

"I can't believe how much I love this little thing. You probably thinkin' your bro's lost it and gone soft, but I tell you that ain't true and Imma get some money and get back to the States and we all gonna be together again. I wish I could take her with me, but she belongs in the trees, so I'm gonna have to let her go as soon as she's big enough to be on her own. And I'm gonna go way out in the woods, like hike all damn day, where there ain't no power lines for her to get electrocuted on or roads she has to cross or stray dogs to get her. You know they don't have, like insulation on the wires down here? It's crazy, animals that live in the trees just trying to get to other trees, but they can't cuz too many trees was cut down, so they use the power lines and can get electrocuted. I mean, like, that's something we don't even think about in the States—insulation on power lines, sssst!" Pablo shakes his head in disappointment, then looks at Calypso with milk all around her mouth, and smiles.

"These kind of sloths you don't see in the zoos back home because they don't live well in captivity—they won't stand to be nobody's slave! I ain't ashamed to say I know I'm gonna cry, but the people who know sloths tell me they're only really happy in the trees and I want her to be happy, you know. I've been doin' a lot of reading about sloths so I can take best care of her, make sure she eats right, learns how to climb, and all that. Yo, I turned by jong into a climbing trainer for her." He turns the camera to a martial arts wooden dummy that's had additional branches and ropes added to it before bringing the camera back. "You know, they got only rod cells in their eyes? That means that . . . like, bright light blinds them like overexposed old-fashioned camera film, so I'm thinking I might try to make some little sunglasses for her. That'd be cute, right? Help her see better in the sunlight." Pablo reaches out for the camera and the video cuts to them sitting outside, with Calypso on her stuffed bear on top of a table with some leaves in front of her.

"I was watchin' some videos and readin' about people who got no cone cells in their eyes—just rods like Calypso—and it looks like I got to make the lenses dark red. Since she can't see red, the red light wouldn't reduce her vision, but just block too much from overwhelming her eyes." He shrugs, then leans back in his chair. Calypso grasps the leaves, opens her mouth wide, and pulls one in.

"I don't know, maybe she won't like 'em, anyway, and there's no good way to hang them on her ears like with us, so I'll have to think of something different."

Calypso stops eating, closes her eyes, and yawns. Pablo continues in a whisper, "OK, she's going to sleep now, so I'm going to put her down and get some stuff done until I gotta feed her again in a few hours. Peace, sis, love you! Say hello to Uncle E!" He reaches a hand for the camera and the video ends.

"So, he was the one who made her those glasses," Miguel says "He also said the same stuff about their eyes that you told me before."

"Well, that's the science," Shriya says.

"Yeah, but I think it's kind of interesting that you both mention it," he says "Not you, maybe, because you're a scientist, but this guy?"

The video over, Shriya closes the laptop. "Think about how we perceive the world so much with our eyes and how that creates our perspective of the world. Sloths don't, they can't. If you want to have any hope of assessing how another animal might understand the world, how it might think and behave, and what its capabilities might be, you need to know its environment, its lifestyle, its body form, and its sensory perceptions." Shriya taps her fingers on the top of the computer, thinking. Then she continues.

"To try to understand something like a sloth, we would need to severely downgrade the importance of one of our most used senses. I think Pablo was doing that, too. It was smart for him to look into people with cone blindness. You're still talking two very different lives and capabilities, but that's as close as you can get when you can't ask a sloth."

"After what I've seen Calypso do," Miguel says, "I'm thinking it's not because they're not smart enough to understand us, it's that we're too dumb to understand them!"

"Funny you say that," Shriya says. "I think animals have some way of communicating that we can't detect."

"Some animals, like dogs, can hear higher pitch noises."

"No, I mean something else. You've spent a lot of time with goats and you've seen these three. Doesn't it seem there's something going on between them that doesn't require sound?" Shriya looks over at Good Boy, who seems to be dreaming of chasing something in his sleep. "Two of them will get up in unison and go out to do something together. We've seen them coordinate attacks against a giant sloth and chimpanzees!"

She holds her palms up in disbelief. "Like, how? And why are some animals instant friends, while some immediately hate each other when there's no prior interaction?"

"Scents maybe?"

"Could be. Dogs perceive the world through smells with the priority we give to vision. Goats also have a better sense of smell."

"You have a theory, though," Miguel says.

"Not really. It's just something I wonder about a lot."

"Hmm." Miguel nods and points to the laptop. "You know, if it weren't for the gang tattoos, I'd never guess that guy was a drug dealer. I don't know why those guys would want to stand out."

"His sister thought he was probably selling guns, but claimed she didn't know what he was involved in. I believe her, but you never know."

"He didn't mention why he named Calypso after a Greek goddess."

"Nymph," says Shriya."

"What's that?"

"Uh, well, I'm not an expert in Greek mythology, but from what I read, the only real difference is that nymphs preside over natural features, like rivers or trees." She waves her hand dismissively. "It doesn't really matter."

"So he did make those sunglasses. He must have been pretty smart." Miguel shakes his head. "What a waste."

"I wish I could have met him," Shriya says quietly." He must have been an interesting guy." Good Boy wakes with a bark and looks around. Shriya and Miguel look at him and he snorts and puts his head back down.

The screen door bangs and Miguel runs over waving his arms, "Hey, I just fixed that!" Juan Manuel runs to the far end of the yard giving off a bleat that's half defiance and half apology. Miguel opens the door and waves to Juan Manuel to call him in.

"Bahahahahahaha," he responds, seeing Shriya and running back to greet her.

"There you are!" Shriya pats the top of his head and checks out his broken horn. "Ow, your horn!" She hugs him and he rests his head on her shoulder.

"Is he going to be OK?" she asks Miguel.

"He should be fine. Everything is healing as it should."

"Did he do this smashing through the door?" she asks.

"No, that was Buca." Miguel sighs and Juan Manuel can sense that the situation is about to get awkward, so he takes a few steps away and looks around for Good Boy. Miguel tells Shriya the story of the two men.

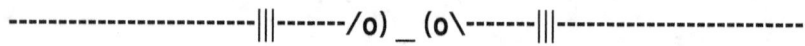

"You just let them take it?" Shriya says with a rising voice.

"If I didn't, they might have killed us all," Miguel insists "They *shot* Charleston's horn off!"

Good Boy looks at Juan Manuel, who turns away. "Don't look at me!" he says, quietly. "I'm a monster!"

"It's just a broken horn."

"Would you say that if you lost an ear?"

"If it got shot off while chasing bad people," Good Boy says, cocking his head, "I'd tell that story to everyone who noticed my missing ear. I'd even point it out if they didn't notice!"

"It's too bad I didn't at least get to knock them into the water," Juan Manuel says. "If *my* ear got shot off, I'd pretend I didn't hear things I didn't want to hear."

"You'd still be able to hear without the flappy part."

"What? I can't hear you!" he jokes.

"Did you at least see what was in the package?" Shriya asks Miguel.

"No, it was just a small box. It was sitting with all the other mail on the table."

"Was it big enough for a journal?"

"Yeah," Miguel says, "it looked like some kind of book, but it wasn't the one he found with us."

Shriya puts her hand to her forehead and blows out a long breath, then she inhales so she can sigh while looking through the rest of the mail. "Why do you think people would come here, threaten you with a gun, and shoot poor Charleston for a package from Rondo?"

Miguel shrugs. "I don't know. They knew about you, though. If you were here, they might have wanted you, too."

Shriya looks up, alarmed. "What did they say about me?"

"They just asked about you and one of them made a dumb joke about Charleston being you and everything they heard about you is a lie."

"What the hell is that supposed to mean?"

"I don't know, maybe Rondo told them you're really attractive?" Miguel lifts and drops his shoulders. "You think Rondo could have found that pirate ship he was looking for?"

"Yes, that's what I think!" she says, frustrated. "And, technically, it was a Spanish treasure ship that was *looted* by pirates."

"I don't need to tell the whole story for you to know what I mean," he responds with some annoyance.

"Yeah, sorry." She puts her hand to her forehead and stares off silently for a moment. "I don't know what else it would be. If it had anything to do with the ancient city after he agreed to leave it alone, Rondo would know better than to reach out to me."

"Maybe the wrong guys found out about it."

Shriya nods her head and turns back to the table. "If he found it, I think it's more likely he's the one who told the wrong people. I don't know how he could salvage it himself, and he told us plainly that he wasn't worried about fighting claims in court, so I have to imagine he wasn't planning on finding help that was concerned about legality and ownership rights."

Miguel nods. "Pirates."

"Basically."

"The kind of guys who'd wonder why they'd need Rondo at all, once they know where the treasure is."

Shriya stares down at the table as if she could have missed something and shakes her head. "Rondo, you arrogant twit! What did you get yourself into?"

"What should we do?" Miguel asks.

"What *can* we do? We don't even know where he'd be."

"Call the authorities?"

"And say what?" Shriya asks.

"OK, I'll admit I'm not a big fan of the guy, but we're just going to let him—"

The excited look on Shriya's face cuts Miguel off and she holds up an envelope, then another, pointing to the return addresses.

"What does it say? Horatio . . . who's that?"

"It's him! Horatio Standish is the character name of his British alter ego back in school."

"Rondo pretended to be British?"

"He was being funny, well *trying* to be funny." Shriya smiles, lost in the past for a moment. "I think he started it to get my attention."

"Sounds like it worked," Miguel says, trying to keep the jealousy out of his voice.

"It did, but it was the wrong kind of attention for him." Shriya opens the first envelope.

"So, you didn't like him, then?"

"No, I couldn't stand him!—know-it-all, arrogant . . ."

"Doesn't sound like he's changed much."

"Yeah, well, that's all just a cover for his insecurity." Shriya looks up from the mail and directly into Miguel's eyes. "I know he can be frustrating, but he's not a bad guy under it all. First time I saw the good part of him was at a party when he got in the middle of what looked like it was going to be a serious fight between two guys over a girl. Somehow, he was able to get the two guys to shake hands and go on their ways and he made sure the drunk girl got home safe."

"Sure, that sounds nice," Miguel concedes. "He probably just got the girl for himself."

"No, I was in the car with them. I don't expect you to like him, but I want you to know he's not a completely terrible person." She reads the letter from the envelope. "And he's not stupid."

"That I knew. What does that letter say?"

"Hm, looks like information on some people." She holds up a couple pieces of paper with the pictures of several men and a brief few sentences about them. "Rondo says to hide this somewhere safe that someone else can get to if anything weird happens, or if we disappear."

"Disappear!" Miguel says, alarmed. "So, *we're* in danger now?!"

Shriya gives a half smile and raises an eyebrow. "I'd say we've been in it since two guys showed up at the door and pulled a gun on you and shot Charleston!"

"It sounded like they had what they wanted and they'd leave us alone."

"At least for now," Shriya says, holding up the photos "These guys look familiar?"

Miguel looks over the grainy, photocopied photos, "No. Definitely not the guys who came here . . . unless they were waiting on the boat. I didn't get a look at them."

Shriya walks over to the small overstuffed bookcase in the living room and takes out the book, *Sloths: From Giant Ground Monsters to Tree-borne Cuteness*, putting the envelope with the information in the back, then sliding it back into its slot in the shelf.

She opens the second envelope and looks at it for a bit before smiling and nodding her head. "So, I don't know what the journal had in it, but I don't think the guys who stole it are going to find what they're looking for."

"Why not?" Miguel asks, moving beside her.

23

"Maybe the book was a decoy, or maybe it had something useful in it, but we have the likely location of the wreck." She holds out the sheet so Miguel can see.

"I don't get it—this is some car rental registration."

"Yeah, except it's not what it looks like." Shriya points out what appears to be two automobile VINs. Her nails are short and ragged, but clean. "These two numbers aren't VINs, they're coordinates."

"How can you tell?" Miguel asks. "They start with 1FA, which isn't part of any kind of navigation I know about."

"I think that's just there so they look like real VINs," Shriya says. "After the 1FA, the first number is one-zero-etc., then there's an N, then the second number: eight-three-etc. I think the N is for *negative*. From where we are, ten degrees latitude, negative eighty-three longitude is not terribly far from here."

"I think you might be right." Miguel squints at it and gets out his phone. He enters the numbers into the GPS and the marker shows up on the coastline only a few hours' drive away. "Whoa, you're a genius!—look!"

"Rondo's the one who thought up the cypher."

"Yeah, but I never would have realized what he did."

"Well, I knew it was from him and he used a fake name only I'd know, so I had to wonder what this was really about— obviously not a rental car form. It also says: *look for the cars at our old office*, and, of course, these *cars* aren't really cars . . . I don't know what else that would mean." Shriya purses her lips and thinks for a moment. "So, yeah, then the numbers just jumped out at me for being familiar."

"That's a really long way of saying, *yes, Miguel, I am a genius.*"

She laughs and kisses him on the cheek.

"Smart women are the sexiest."

"Oh, yeah?" She raises an eyebrow and kisses him on the lips.

Click goes the latch for Calypso's door and she climbs her way inside. The spring loaded door shuts behind her.

Miguel sighs in disappointment.

Shriya smiles at him and taps the end of his nose. "You can't have me without the kids."

"I know," Miguel says, "and it's time for their animal show."

Shriya uses a clothespin to hang some leaves and hibiscus flowers from the rope above the couch, but Calypso holds out her arm for Shriya to carry her instead. Juan Manuel and Good Boy sitting on the floor between them and the TV.

Miguel sits down next to Shriya on the couch with Calypso holding onto her and her head turned around at the television. "How do you think they always know what time it is?" he asks Shriya.

"Position of the sun? I don't know, but it *is* the only thing on their schedule."

Raccoons. Good Boy barks at their appearance on the TV and looks at Shriya and Calypso. Calypso looks at Good Boy, then up at Shriya, then back at the TV. Sometimes Good Boy's not very smart, but she keeps it to herself.

Shriya laughs. "I wonder if he thinks it looks like a sloth?" she says, looking at Good Boy.

"That's a raccoon," she tells him, "They do kind of look alike with the bands around their eyes, but look how fast they are!"

"You've never seen a raccoon?" Juan Manuel asks Good Boy.

"I've never seen most of the animals on here," Good Boy growls softly. "Where did you see one?"

"They live around. Usually out at night."

"Maybe I've smelled one."

"Probably," Juan Manuel tells him. "They stink."

"OK, but can't you see that if sloths were fast, they'd probably be like raccoons?"

"No."

"Ah, forget it." Good Boy turns back to the TV.

"They have a tail and ears!" Juan Manuel tells Good Boy. "The only thing that's similar is the black streaks around the eyes."

"And they're clever," says Good Boy.

Juan Manuel snorts. "So are monkeys."

"There's no need for that kind of talk, Juan Manuel!" Calypso scolds.

When the animal show ends, Shriya changes to a history program about pirates. Miguel puts his arm around Shriya, Good Boy yawns and sighs, Juan Manuel decides to go back outside, and Calypso climbs onto the rope to head back to the trees. When she turns to looks at the TV one last time, she sees a man holding the end of a stick up to his eye while standing on a platform at the top of a tree that reminds her of the lookout towers the giant monkeys used in the lost city.

He yells down the tree and the view pulls back to show that the tree has two companions in a line, and these trees only have a few very straight limbs that stick out to each side. Stretched from the tree trunks like the web of a spider that would have to be as big as Thundersloth, are the vines that people make, but thicker. Hanging from the tree limbs are enormous leaves unlike any Calypso has ever eaten.

The view pulls back farther and points down to show that the trees are growing out of a boat and the boat is moving upon the big water and catching up to a smaller boat that only has one tree growing out of it. Now the view is on the big boat and an angry-looking man in an unusual hat stands behind a large wheel and yells at other people that scamper around and climb the webs like monkeys. Calypso decides to stay and learn more about this strange tree boat.

As the big boat approaches the smaller one, the view shifts to its side and large guns poke out of holes. Fire and smoke puff out of them and the water around the small boat splashes up in massive spouts. The small boat slows down for the big boat to pull up alongside and angry people jump from the big boat to the small one filled with frightened people. Then the view changes to a person talking at her, but Calypso doesn't understand much of what he's saying. The person must be talking to Shriya and Miguel, but they have their mouths against each other and aren't paying attention. Good Boy stares at the screen with his head glued to the floor trying to ignore what's happening on the couch.

Calypso thinks it's nice of this person to try to explain things to her, so she doesn't want to climb away while he's talking, but there's only so long she can stand it before she starts to make her way toward her door. Then the boats are back and she stops to watch again. She hangs from her feet and scratches her belly. The angry people move all kinds of boxes off the small boat and onto the big boat, and then they leave the small boat. And now the man is back to talk, but he doesn't seem to notice that nobody's paying attention to him. She waits to see if the boats show up again and daydreams about climbing the trees on a boat. The big boat seems much slower than the boat she drives, which sounds more appealing.

Now the people are on land somewhere in the kind of place where people live close together and there aren't enough trees. The angry man with the odd hat is there, but he doesn't look angry anymore. A female person is sitting on his lap and drinking something.

Shriya pulls away from Miguel for a moment. "Hey, did you hear that?"

"What?" Miguel asks.

"They're talking about Captain Williamson, one of the pirates Rondo was talking about."

Miguel picks up the remote, fumbles it, and turns up the volume.

The people love noise, Calypso thinks.

The TV narrator goes on: *"So, Louis LeFleur joined up with Captain Williamson, and their combined pirate fleet sailed the Caribbean, gathering together a king's fortune in treasure and a small navy's worth of men eager to join their crews. With the Royal Navy stretched thin fighting the War of Spanish Succession, the generally smaller war ships available to counter the pirate scourge spent their time alternately in pursuit or running away depending upon how the winds or their number of guns favored them. Unfortunately for the Navy, Captain Williamson was a particularly masterful sailor and the Royal Navy officers at the time more often received their commissions through family political connections than their skill. Like many pirate crews, the men—and several women—of Williamson's fleet were quite diverse, with people from many cultures: freed African slaves, indigenous Americans, Pacific Islanders, and even some Inuit whose nearly silent sealskin kayaks came to good use for sneaking up on British warships to sabotage them in the middle of the night, for slipping in and out of a town for a surprise raid, or even to use as small fire ships when lashed together and rigged with a rudimentary sail."*

"Sounds pretty much like what Rondo said," Miguel says.

"Yeah, he knows his stuff."

"In the epic ten-hour battle between the ships of Commander Blackburn of the Royal Navy and Williamson's pirate fleet, Louis LeFleur's ship, Frères de la Liberté, *was one of several which were sunk. Around the fourth hour of battle, LeFleur had just sent the stricken* HMS Bountiful *to the bottom and was in the middle of making a turn to assist one of Williamson's sloops when his magazine took a direct hit, reducing the ship to splinters. Legend says that LeFleur was blown onto the top of his mainmast and, as it slid through the bottom of the hull into the inferno, he saluted Williamson's ship,* Duchess.*"*

Calypso watches the reenactment of LeFleur's dramatic legendary death and munches a hibiscus flower.

"With the loss of the Frères de la Liberté *and the declining wind, Williamson's remaining fleet consisting of his unique 32-gun galley and three sloops of varying arms, was outgunned by Blackburn's frigate,* HMS Ipswich, *and his accompanying three sloops-of-war. As he could no longer rely on their generally*

better seafaring skills to outmaneuver the British Navy, he resorted to his unique flag code to indicate for general retreat and to meet up at Big Corn Island.

Unusual for the time and considered outdated, Duchess *was a galley, which allowed the crew to row into the wind to flee the battle."*

Calypso wonders why she's never seen boats like these. She's seen a few small ones with the giant leaves, but nothing like the big ones with so many trees growing out of them. The thought had never occurred to her that there could be moving trees.

"Unfortunately for Williamson and his pirates, Commander Blackburn had been able to take several pirates prisoner, one of whom relayed the location of where the remaining fleet was to regroup, setting up the ambush that would result in the famous last stand of Williamson and with it, the last hope of the Scottish colony of New Caledonia in modern day Panama and a naval presence in the Caribbean."

Calypso sniffs up and down the rope. She's all out of hibiscus flowers and she has to poop, so she decides to go back outside. She doesn't hear the rest of the people's conversation.

"I think we should take Buca with us in case we need him," Shriya says and Good Boy puts his ears on alert.

"Not Charleston and Calypso?" Miguel asks with a laugh.

"I think they've been through more than enough dangers. They should be fine here. I'll leave word with Maria to keep an eye on them and the place."

"Who's Ramon Santiago?" Miguel asks, looking at the signature name on the letter from Rondo, now back out and lying on the coffee table.

Shriya looks at where he's pointing at the letter. "I don't know. Could just be a made up name, but that's a good question."

"Yeah, I wonder," Miguel nods, getting up and going to the computer in the next room on the kitchen table.

"Shriya, you might want to read this," Miguel says after a moment, and Shriya goes over to the computer.

"*In 1865, spiritualist, Ramon Santiago, believing he had spoken to the dead pirate captain, Louis LeFleur in a dream, set out to follow his supernatural instructions to locate the lost gold of the Spanish treasure galleon, the* Santa Teresa de Avila, *in order to prove that people can talk to the dead as well as make himself rich,*" Miguel reads aloud to her. "*The pirate had learned about the wreck of the* Santa Teresa *after coming upon one of her sister ships that had been left drifting after a terrible storm and the survivors told him about how she had been lost upon the rocks at the footing of a small fort whose location has been lost to time.*"

Shriya reaches out and scrolls through the parts she now knows and reads some more to Miguel.

"*A friend of Ramon claimed that Ramon showed him some encrusted silver coins that he said were from the* Santa Teresa. *According to the friend, Ramon stated that much of the contents of the wreck had been buried by the collapse of the fort during the same storm and that he was tunneling his way through the rock to reach it. When his friend offered to help, Ramon refused, but promised him a portion of the treasure in exchange for keeping quiet about his find. The friend had his son attempt to follow Ramon back to the wreck site, but seemingly aware or just paranoid, Ramon took a long circuitous route to lose him and that was the last anyone saw of Ramon. Rumors eventually started that the son had killed Ramon while trying to get the information of the wreck site from him and the son and father were questioned by authorities, but they were released for lack of any evidence. Other theories on what happened to Ramon include death by tropical disease or animals, that he was killed while trying to dynamite through the rock, and even one dismissed by most historians that he had recovered the treasure and retired with his wealth to Jamaica under an assumed identity.*"

Good Boy comes running into the kitchen, barking and growling..

"What's going on?" Miguel asks him with worry, hearing the sound of angry dogs outside. Shriya jumps up from her seat.

Juan Manuel sees three medium sized dogs surrounding Calypso at the bottom of a tree. He yells and races across the yard, charging the canines, but they dodge him with a laugh and encircle him.

"Cabrito has a broken horn!" one of the dogs laughs.

"That's funny—a goat threatening us! Do you really think you can take on three dogs, cabrito?"

"If three's all you've got!" Juan Manuel shakes his head and stands up on two legs. Calypso climbs the tree as fast as she can. The three dogs lunge, Juan Manuel comes down, head butting one of them, stunning him and throwing him backwards, but the other two dogs sink their teeth into Juan Manuel's back legs. Hopping and kicking to shake them off, only gets them to dig in even more.

The stunned dog recovers and smiles, baring his fangs, "That's all *you've* got? I was hoping for a fight."

Good Boy lands behind them from a leap off the porch railing and snarls, "I'm your huckleberry." The two other dogs release Juan Manuel and square up to Good Boy, who slashes the first dog's nose with his teeth and immediately turns to bite hard into the throat of the second. The third lunges, but Good Boy lets go of the second dog to slice the third in the face, cutting through his eye.

The half-blinded dog howls and the first dog clamps onto Good Boy's leg, but he's too stupid to let go and Good Boy pulls him closer to his mouth to tear into his throat and shake him. Juan Manuel back-kicks the second dog before he can come back at Good Boy, sending him skidding and running off whining, then he whips his horn at the third dog, who dodges the strike.

Good Boy flings the lifeless body of the first dog from his mouth and growls at the remaining dog, who freezes with fear long enough for Juan Manuel to throw his head back into his side, puncturing his chest with his intact horn and tossing him through the air. Severely injured, but powered by adrenaline, it runs away, trailing blood. Good Boy would chase him, but his leg hurts.

"Next time, bring more friends!" he barks after him. Miguel comes running up with his rifle, futilely pointing it at the dead dog. Good Boy and Juan Manuel look at him, then each other. Shriya comes running up as well.

"This guy!" Good Boy says, shaking his head.

"He's a hero," Juan Manuel snorts and looks up at Calypso. She looks down at him and blinks a thank you.

"Dogs?" Shriya asks Miguel. She has a dented, pointed spade in her hand.

"Yeah, two or three of them were attacking Charleston. Good Boy jumped in. Judging by Calypso only being a few meters up the tree, I would bet they were after her and Charleston stepped in to protect her first."

Shriya looks down at the dog Good Boy killed and checks it out. "Well, this one's dead."

"Another one ran away as I opened the door, and a third before I reached the bottom of the stairs. Charleston got him pretty good with his horn."

Shriya follows the blood trail to the street with her eyes. "Must be a pretty severe wound." She grimaces and stabs the shovel into the ground. "They came against my family, so they got what they deserve." She bends down and puts her arms around Juan Manuel and Good Boy and pats them, "Such heroic animals! I am so lucky to have you living here with me!"

She stands up to reach for Calypso, who looks up the tree and back at her, then back up the tree, then comes down a little and holds her arm out to be picked up.

"Do you think they're strays?" Miguel asks, looking down at the dead dog's frayed, bloody collar.

"No," Shriya says, angrily, "these are the dogs of that jerk down the street."

"The crazy guy?"

"Yeah," Shriya says, and nudges the dead dog with her toe. "We should drop this one off at his front door."

"I don't know if it's a good idea to make a guy like that angry," Miguel says. "I'll dump it in the river and wash some of this blood off the ground."

Shriya nods. "Or let him come here and we can dump *him* in the river."

"I think that's a little too drastic, don't you?" Miguel says, a little surprised at Shriya's ferocity. "I doubt those dogs will be back. If they survive. But what was that you were saying about the animals being safer here?"

"Yeah, maybe we'll take them with us." Shriya looks at Good Boy and Charleston's legs. "But, first we're taking them to get looked at and stitched up. I thought this was just the dog's blood on Charleston, but I think the end of his broken horn might be bleeding again and they've both got some bites on them."

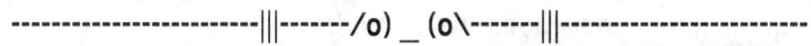

Shriya parks her car and Calypso is happy to be able to soon get back in the trees after such a long day of monster dogs and a veterinary clinic waiting room full of overly friendly people who all wanted to touch her when all she wanted to do was hug her friends and be home. Juan Manuel can't wait to eat. Good Boy feels fine—the people stitched him and put a bandage on his wound, but he didn't need it. He's supposed to be wearing a goofy cone around his neck, but there's no way anyone's putting it on him and, so far, nobody's tried too hard to make him wear it. Juan Manuel got some bandages, but no stitches. When they get out of the car, a smell hits Good Boy, and he doesn't feel so fine anymore—it's the people who shot Juan Manuel. The fur on his back stands on end and he growls to get everyone's attention.

"What is it, Buca?" Shriya asks, kneeling down.

"Bad men!" he barks back.

Miguel looks at the house and down at Good Boy, who barks up at him and at the house. "I wonder if those guys might have come back," he says to Shriya.

Shriya stares at the house. "Yeah. I'm wondering that, too."

"I'm going to go around the side and see if there's another boat on the dock," Miguel says, starting to move. "Stay by the car."

"Be careful!" Shriya says, touching his arm.

Good Boy starts to follow, but realizes Shriya isn't going along, so he stays with her.

"Should I go with him?" Juan Manuel asks.

"If you want to." Good Boy says, standing tensely beside Shriya. "I'm staying with her and Calypso."

"Yeah, me too." Juan Manuel says, as he watches Miguel slip down the overgrown alley along the far side of the neighbor's house and around behind it. He immediately feels like he should have gone with Miguel in case the bad people are in there. A few minutes later, Miguel sticks his head out the front door holding a rifle in his hand, and waves them inside.

Shriya lets Calypso go on the rope and she climbs toward the outside door for the trees at her top speed. The place is even messier now—furniture overturned, books knocked off the shelf, and all the drawers in the kitchen pulled out of their cabinets and dumped onto the floor.

"Must have been them. Who else would have trashed the place?" Shriya says. "And nothing seems missing. They even left the TV and the computer."

"They went through that, too," Miguel says.

"What's that?" She looks at the screen to see that it was left open on her email.

"I told you to use a password."

"Then they would have taken the computer to see if they could hack into it," Shriya says in aggravated defeat. "There was nothing in there from Rondo, if that's what they were looking for."

She turns toward the bookcase in the other room, but the shelf where the book hiding Rondo's letters resides is largely intact and the book is still there. She goes over and retrieves the letters.

"There *is* something missing," Miguel says with trepidation.

"What's that?"

"The boat's gone."

"My Zodiac?!"

"No, the speedboat, but—"

"What?!" Shriya bolts out the back door, leaps down the stairs, and runs to the dock, looking down the river for the thieves. Good Boy follows, barking, pacing up and down the dock in frustration. The Speedwell is gone and her rigid inflatable boat is now floppy and half deflated from stab wounds to the tubes.

Miguel catches up and Juan Manuel limps in behind.

"Who the hell are these guys?" she screams, steam practically coming off of her head.

"I can patch it," Miguel frowns at the Zodiac.

"So can I!" she yells, and then takes a deep breath and apologizes before untying the boat, which Miguel helps her guide up onto the lawn. "They stole Calypso's boat! I can't replace that. Those Speedwells are really expensive if you order them, and I don't have the time or tools to build one from a kit. Even if I had the money, how am I going to ask them to build one with the sloth-friendly controls? Pablo's probably the one who built it, and he's dead."

"I mean, she seems totally fine with her tree."

"Calypso is a sloth that drives a speedboat. One of the world's slowest animals with terrible vision operates a *speed*boat, Miguel," Shriya says, the edge back in her voice. "That's . . . it's mental! Calypso needs to have her boat. I mean, it's the least we can do for her after she rescued us how many times?" Shriya looks around her feet and, finding a small stone, picks it up, and whips it out into the river with a scream of frustration.

She closes her eyes and takes a deep breath with her arms at her side. When she opens her eyes, she's calm again. "I

35

can't even believe what my life has become that that sentence came out of my face, serious and sober!"

"OK, sorry, but what can we do?" Miguel asks. "These are some bad dudes. Are you a trained soldier? I'm not."

"No, but are we pushovers?" She points at him. "You know what we're going to do? We're going to ten degrees something latitude, negative eighty whatever longitude and we're going to get any treasure that's there before they do, even if I have to talk to the ghosts of Louis LeFleur and Ramon . . . whoever!"

"Santiago."

"Yeah, him!"

"Oh, good. For a moment there, I thought you were going to suggest something crazy."

"You can stay here." Shriya says, lifting her arms out to her sides and dropping them back.

Miguel shrugs. "Nah, my life is too boring. I'll call my cousin and tell him to take care of the goats."

Highwaymen

The bags are in the trunk, the friends are in the back seat, and the people are in the front of Shriya's beat up, but unstoppable old Toyota Corolla, heading for the coast. The back is crowded and Calypso has her sunglasses on and is hanging off the back of Miguel's seat with her head out the window to feel the wind in her fur and to keep her nose in the stream of clean air because *somebody* ate something that's trying to get revenge upon everyone else.

"Somebody really ate some farts for lunch," Miguel complains.

"Whomever smelt it, dealt it," Shriya says.

"Maybe it was Calypso, which is why she's hanging behind me trying to make me look guilty."

"It couldn't be her."

"Oh, that's right, ladies don't fart!"

Shriya laughs. "Of course that's not true! No, *sloths* don't fart. I think it's Buca. It might be from the blood of that dog he killed."

"Yeah, he's some dog, that's for sure," Miguel says. "It looked like he was taking on three of them at once, though Charleston gave him a some help."

Juan Manuel frowns and looks at Good Boy.

"You're a good assistant, goat." Good Boy says with a smile.

Juan Manuel makes a fart noise at him with his mouth.

"I think that one came from the goat," Miguel says.

Shriya looks in the rear-view mirror and smiles at Juan Manuel. "He does that with his mouth when he's been insulted."

"Who insulted him?"

"You! You only credited him with an assist when he skewered one of those dogs with his horn. I'll bet that one didn't make it home. Buca is a trained attack dog, but you should recognize just how tough Charleston is, too."

Miguel raises his eyebrows. "He doesn't know what I'm saying!"

"You're going to go with that after everything we've seen these animals do?"

Miguel nods and turns to Juan Manuel. "Sorry, Charleston, I know you're a macho goat."

"Bahahahahaha," he responds, which sounds a lot nicer to the people who don't understand what he really means.

Shriya checks the cracked side view mirror. "Is that white sedan back there the same one that was behind us earlier?"

Miguel checks his mirror, which he has adjusted for his seat. "No, that's a Toyota. The other one was a Nissan."

"Are you sure?"

"Yeah, this one also has a blue scrape on the bumper." Miguel assures her. "I don't think you can see it from your side."

"Well, the crack in the mirror doesn't help, either."

"Then don't hit stuff!"

"You mean don't park it anywhere other people might drive by?"

Miguel nods. "Exactly. What are you doing on public roads?—people are crazy!"

As if on cue, a car cuts right in front of them and brakes hard to make a turn, forcing Shriya to brake and turn a little to avoid a collision.

"This is why I drive a big truck," Miguel says, adjusting his seatbelt from where it has tightened.

Shriya laughs and grabs his chin. "I hate to break it to you, but in the US, your truck would be considered a kiddie ride."

"Yeah, well I don't have a bulldozer to drive in front of me to clear a path. It's such a big place, huh?"

"The US?"

"Yeah."

"Mostly. It's a big country, so it varies," Shriya says. Petrol is cheap and in some of the flat areas where everything's far apart and the roads are wide and straight, a big truck kind of makes sense. I would never want one of those in a city, but people do it. I don't think you could get away with it in a lot of other countries."

"I'd like to see it," Miguel says wistfully.

"Which part?"

"I don't know. Los Angeles, maybe? Miami. The Grand Canyon. Did you see those places?"

"No. I had a holiday in Florida once, but I didn't get to Miami. I've been to LA for a conference and I visited the La Brea Tar Pits."

"Is LA like the movies?" Miguel asks.

"Kind of. Some of it almost seems like a movie set, but that might just be because it's in so many movies. Traffic is terrible. The Tar Pits were fascinating, though, even when I thought I knew what to expect."

```
         /\      /\                                      ~ \   / ~
_____  \ 0 \    0 /   ----------|||--/o) _ (o\--|||--------  (     )  _____
          \     /                                          \_/
           \   /
            \_/
```

Traffic thins out as they get closer to the town nearest their destination. Shriya discretely checks the mirrors again. "That white car is still there, Miguel."

"Yeah, it's starting to worry me, too. We can't have it follow us to the hotel."

"Exactly. What do you think I should do?"

"I don't know," Miguel says, sounding a little worried. "I've only seen movies and I don't think a car chase ending with the bad guy crashing into a parked car, flying through the air, and exploding is going to work here."

"That would be pretty brilliant, though."

"But *maybe* he's just some guy going the same way."

"How do we tell?" Shriya asks.

"Pull over and see if they do the same then ask them if they're following us?"

"And they might answer with a bullet."

"Nah," Miguel says, looking back at Juan Manuel with a grin, "we'll have the goat fight them off."

"Maybe I'll just take four right turns to make a circle and see if they're still behind us."

"Yeah, that's a better idea."

Juan Manuel perks his head up from the back seat and looks at Good Boy crammed into the foot well. "Was he making fun of me?"

"I think so, I wasn't really listening."

"I think he was mocking me."

"Probably was."

"You're no help."

"I've never kept it secret that I'm not fond of him."

"Yeah," Juan Manuel says, "I just thought it was because you were jealous."

"It can be more than one reason."

"Ha! You admit it, then."

Good Boy raises his head then lowers it. "OK, you got me."

"And now I'll never mention it again."

"I should've said it sooner."

"That car is still behind us," Shriya says as they make the third right turn.

"Pull over," Miguel tells her, "and leave enough room so you can pull out in a hurry."

"Good idea."

Forced to either pass them or reveal themselves, the suspicious car drives by.

"They won't even look at us even though I'm staring at them. A normal person would look back wondering why I'm staring."

Miguel opens his door.

40

"What are you doing?"

"Looking like we're getting out so maybe they go around the block and wait for us, but that will give us time to get some distance instead."

"I was thinking I'll just follow *them* for a while," Shriya says.

"I don't know if it's a good idea. If they're not following us, it's a waste of time and if they are, we don't know what they might do."

"What are they going to do?"

He looks at her. "I don't know. That's why I said we don't know!"

"Don't pull an attitude on me."

"I'm not, but I feel like you don't really listen to me."

"I listen to you," Shriya sighs. "I just . . . .. Yeah, sorry."

"It's OK. I think it's better if we don't show our hand unless we have to."

The suspicious car turns the corner, Miguel shuts the door, and Shriya nods and pulls back into the traffic. "You're right," she admits. "I wish we had the giant sloth here to rip the roof off their car and find out what they're doing."

"What if they're not really following us?"

"Then they'll have a roadster," she says with a shrug and a smile.

The rest of the drive is uneventful with Shriya pulling an occasional circle to detect any cars that might be following. Miguel calls it a "Crazy Ivan" then explains the potentially dangerous Soviet Cold War submariner practice of using sudden sharp turns to hear if an enemy ship had been hiding in the sonar blind spot behind their submarine.

"Where did you learn about that?" Shriya asks.

"Movies. *The Hunt for Red October*."

"I never saw that one. Is it good?"

"I think you'd like it," Miguel says. "It's more a strategy kind of thing than an outright action movie."

"I don't mind action movies, I just don't like the ones that are all ridiculous action with no plot or character development."

"What are they talking about?" Calypso asks Juan Manuel with a yawn from the back of a sleeping Good Boy.

"I don't know, but I wish we'd just get where we're going already."

Calypso listens to the music playing through the speakers in the door. "Is this a song about monkeys?"

"Yes, someone is warning another person that there's a monkey on their back."

"They have to sing a whole song about that?"

"Why not?" Juan Manuel asks. "Monkeys are dangerous. Well, the big ones with spears are."

"That's the reason not to sing about them!"

"There's a bunch of other words, too. I think it's a warning to watch out for monkeys."

"Oh, that makes sense. Good advice," Calypso says. "Though they're not all bad."

Juan Manual nods, receiving a sharp pain from his broken horn that he ignores. "It's a good thing, too, or we wouldn't have made it out of that city in the jungle."

"Yes." With another yawn, Calypso closes her eyes and goes back to sleep.

"I haven't heard George Michael in a while," Miguel says.

"Get used to it," Shriya says. "This is my '80s mix."

"I'm not complaining, though I can't speak for the animals." He looks back to see them all with their eyes closed. "They seem too sleepy to care."

The Hotel Hispaniola

Miguel gets a room at the Hotel Hispaniola while Shriya takes the animals for a much-needed walk. The boredom and hunger of the car ride is forgotten by Juan Manuel within minutes of being able to stretch his sore legs and eat some of the random vegetation he finds in a wooded area behind the hotel. Shriya goes to put Calypso on a tree, but Calypso doesn't let go of her shirt.

"You must be hungry!" Shriya encourages her. Calypso stretches her arm toward a different tree and Shriya brings her to that one.

"Ah, you're just very selective, there's nothing wrong with that—you don't want to just settle for whatever tree just happens to . . . be there . . ." Shriya trails off with a sigh.

A small off road vehicle parks in the far side of the dirt lot. The door opens and the scent of a female dog gets Good Boy's attention. He turns to see a Belgian Malinois with the most perfect shiny brown coat of even color and a black face with elegantly pointed ears—alert, inquisitive, nearly forming a heart-shape with her nose. Her eyes scan the area for threats in a particular way—she's been through attack training, too! The eyes turn to him and stop for a moment, nearly drawing the breath out of his body.

"Hi, my name is Good Boy," he says quietly. Then her eyes pass on by.

"What?" Juan Manuel eating nearby asks.

"Nothing."

Juan Manuel follows his gaze and sees the other dog. Her master walks to the hotel and she follows with hardly a look back. "Ah. Pretty interesting looking for a dog. Too bad she doesn't seem interested in you."

"Yeah, yeah, goat," Good Boy says with annoyance. "Too bad a dog didn't dump in that grass you're eating."

Juan Manuel chuckles.

43

The old AC hisses and moans like the ghost of an arthritic lizard, but whatever it's complaining about, it isn't the work it's been tasked with, since it isn't performing any. Finally more tired of hearing it than he is from the drive and the spray-adhesive air, Miguel gets out of bed and shuts the AC off. The window screens are intact, so he opens the windows to let the outside humidity mingle with the inside humidity, get married, and have kids to saturate the air to what he figures must be the level just short of forming a storm cloud.

Winged insects or pterodactyls try their best to tear through the netting and consume them all and leave nothing but skeletons behind. The outdoor sounds of birds, insects, monkeys, and what might be a demon looking for damned souls fills the room, but it still beats the tortured wraith of a once proud AC unit.

"Listen to them, the children of the night. What lovely music they make." Shriya says, laying on her back on top of the bedcovers in a thin tank top and shorts that feel like shrink wrap, arms outstretched to maximize cooling.

"Ah, that *fresh* humid air is so much better than the stale humidity," Miguel complains sarcastically.

Good Boy gets up and climbs into the tub to sleep—ah, the refreshing coolness of the hard porcelain! It smells funny in here, he thinks. No, it's not *funny*, it's just . . . what *is* that smell? He tries unsuccessfully to shake it out of his nose. At least it's cooler in here.

Calypso sleeps soundly at the foot of Shriya's bed, and Juan Manuel had been comfortably sleeping on the floor until Miguel woke him up. He looks around for Good Boy and finds him in the bathroom. He decides to sleep on the hard but cool tile floor.

Asleep, but never completely at rest, Good Boy's ears pick up something that kick-starts his brain. Head up, full alert, he listens carefully over the noise of those children of the night . . . there it is! He hops out of the tub and trots to the hotel room door. Everyone else is fast asleep.

A floorboard creaks outside like something being sneaky, trying not to make it creak. If they weren't up to no good, they'd be less careful about making noise. As Good Boy fixes his senses on the door, a light foot stops right outside. Then . . . nothing. But he knows there's someone there and they're not fooling him. His heart beats faster and he wonders if he should wake everyone, or if whatever's on the other side of the door will go away.

Noises from the door—a key pushing itself past the pins of the old deadbolt lock, one at a time. Good Boy starts with a low growl that can be felt as much as heard. The sound stops, so he does, too. Your move, bad guy. A few interminably long moments pass. The lock clicks and the deadbolt slides quietly away from its reinforced pocket in the doorjamb. The doorknob starts to turn.

Juan Manuel now steps up quietly behind him. Good Boy motions with his head for him to take the doorknob side of the doorway and get ready for a fight. Juan Manuel rises onto his back legs in anticipation and Good Boy steps out of the door's opening arc, ready to jump on whatever comes through that door be it man, bear, or jaguar.

"What is it?" Shriya whispers. Good Boy looks back at her and she shakes Miguel awake.

"What?" he asks loudly, and whoever is outside swiftly releases the doorknob and withdraws the key. Footsteps run into the distance. Shriya leaps from the bed and pulls open the door. Good Boy and Juan Manuel rush around her to beat her outside. A car roars off from somewhere behind the building next door. They look around for a few moments, but don't see anyone.

"What do you think that was about—random thief or someone who was trying to find something specific?" Shriya asks.

"Maybe just random," Miguel says, looking around the parking lot. "We lost the guys that might have been following us."

"Did we?"

"If it was them, why would they run? They would have had the drop on us."

"I don't know, but I don't like it." Shriya says. "Buca, Charleston, come on inside." She locks the door and jams it shut with a wooden chair of sub-optimal rigidity under the doorknob.

Good Boy sits on the floor, staring at the door just in case.

"What happened?" asks a sleepy Calypso from the bed.

"Someone bad tried to come in." Good Boy growls.

"Good thing we have you!"

He starts to turn to her, but thinks again and trains his eyes on the door.

The next morning, they go for a walk to get breakfast and find the man from the parking lot the day before at the same place with the Belgian Malinois tied up outside. Shriya leashes Good Boy and Juan Manuel to a post just out of reach, in case the new dog isn't friendly. Calypso sits on Good Boy's back and Shriya scratches her under the chin.

"I'll see if I can get you all some kind of treats," she tells them. "I know you'll keep everyone safe, Buca." She gives the other dog a wary eye, but it only sits and stares at her like a stone carving with judging eyes. Must be another trained attack dog, Shriya thinks, looking back at Good Boy—another statue— and she and Miguel go inside the restaurant.

"You should talk to her," Juan Manuel says quietly.

"And say what?"

"I don't know, ask her if she's ever seen a giant stink sloth or been in a speedboat."

"Why would I ask that?" Good Boy says.

"Because you want to start a conversation."

"Yeah, but I don't want to sound like I'm trying to start a conversation."

"Then how do you expect to have one?"

"I don't know, I need an opening that isn't weird."

"How about: hi, my name is Good Boy, do you like my backpack?"

"I need a *good* opening that isn't weird," Good Boy says.

"I'm not a backpack," Calypso protests.

"That's why it's funny," Juan Manuel insists.

"What's the funny part?"

"If I have to explain it, you don't get it."

"If you have to explain it," Calypso says, "it's not funny. When I'm interested, I only have to call out and they come to me."

"Nice to be a sloth sometimes," Good Boy frowns.

"What if more than one show up?" Juan Manuel asks.

"They try to throw each other out of the tree. The weak ones get thrown out of the tree and the smart ones find a way past while another two fight it out."

"I never thought that sloths fight over mates like the rest of us."

"Just like anyone else, we wouldn't want a weak mate and end up with weak babies that might not survive."

"What about the smart ones? They might not be the strongest, but they would win." Good Boy asks.

"Yes. For sloths, smart is better than strong."

"Your mother must have preferred the smart ones," Good Boy says.

"Yes."

"Hey, she's looking over here," Juan Manuel interrupts.

Good Boy turns slightly toward the Belgian Malinois and nods.

"I'm Zonda," the Malinois says, her mouth opening wide to display shining teeth under a long, elegant nose. "What's a Buca?"

Juan Manuel leans towards Calypso, "Maybe you might want to—"

"Yup," Calypso grabs his good horn and pulls herself onto his back.

"It's shortened from Bucephalus."

Zonda laughs in a rhythmic exhalation, and then asks, "What is that name?"

Good Boy might have been offended if her laugh wasn't so beautiful. "It was the name of a great war horse that some warrior person rode."

"You're named after a horse?" Zonda laughs again. "Is it because the sloth rides on your back like a person? Is the sloth a great warrior?"

Good Boy looks at Calypso and back at Zonda. "You'd be surprised."

Zonda nods and gives him a sideways glance, "Maybe I would. Those are some big claws she has."

Calypso holds one of her arms up and opens her mouth in an attempt at a menacing pose that Zonda takes as comedic. "We don't call him that silly name," Calypso says, "We call him Good Boy."

"What's a Zonda?" Good Boy asks her, hoping to guide the conversation back to her.

"It's a fast wind that comes off the mountains."

"Wow, that's a good one," he nods. "Wow, yeah, that's a really nice name."

"Thank you," she says, ducking her head. When she speaks again, she leans toward him with her head turned a bit away. "Are you really a good boy?"

"Sometimes," Good Boy smiles.

"He is!" Calypso says. "He's the best boy there is!"

Zonda laughs again, turning fully away, and Good Boy gives Calypso a look of disapproval to get her to stop helping. Juan Manuel chuckles.

Calypso blinks slowly and reconsiders her apparent social faux pas. "No, he's actually the worst. He eats puppies, and poops in the people's shoes and—"

Good Boy closes his eyes in embarrassment. "Please stop," he says quietly.

"Fine," Calypso says back to him, "I don't know what I should say."

"Don't say anything."

"What happened to your leg?" Zonda asks, pretending not to hear the conversation.

Good Boy sits up a little straighter. "Fought off a pack of dogs."

"Is that what happened to you, too, goat?"

"I'm Juan Manuel."

"Hello, Juan Manuel."

"Yeah, I confronted the dogs first."

"*You* did? A whole pack of dogs?"

"Yes, and Good Boy finished them!"

"They broke your horn off?"

"No," Juan Manuel says self-consciously.

"A bad person shot him with a gun," Good Boy says.

"Does it hurt?" she asks Juan Manuel.

"Only most of the time."

She winces in empathy. "Do horns grow back like claws?"

"I heard both that they do and that they don't. I'll find out."

"You're an impressive bunch," Zonda says as her person comes out and unties her. "Maybe I'll see you all again," she says as they walk away.

"Yeah, we go on adventures all over, so you never can tell!" Good Boy shouts, shaking his head, then turning to Calypso. "Why did you say those things?"

"I was trying to help and you didn't like when I said you were the best, so I went the other way."

"I poop in people's shoes?" Good Boy says, incredulously, "That was going to help?"

"I was trying to think of what the people would think is bad and..." Calypso scratches herself, ". . . yeah, I don't know where that came from." She shakes her head, "Sorry, I'll fix it if we see her again."

"Please don't try to fix it!" Good Boy says. "Leave it to me. If I need help . . ." He lowers his head and blows a sigh out of his nose, "Ah, she's higher in the pack, anyway."

"What does that mean?" Calypso asks.

"It means he thinks she's better than him," Juan Manuel explains.

"Why would he think that?"

"It's a social thing. We have levels in a pack or herd," Juan Manuel tells her. "Some individuals are more liked or respected than others and those are considered to be higher up. The weaker or less popular members don't mingle with them."

"What herd?" Calypso says. "No one was here but us! She's either interested or she isn't, it doesn't have anything to do with some weird herd thing."

Good Boy manages to mutter, "It's a pack when you're talking about dogs."

"Herd, pack, flock, mob, swarm—you're the best in any group of any dogs anywhere. Everywhere! And why are there so many words for a group?"

Good Boy sighs. "Thanks. I'm not so sure you're right, but thanks."

"Of course I'm right, don't be silly."

Good Boy meets Juan Manuel's eyes. "Well, that didn't go how I wanted."

"Why's that?" Juan Manuel asks.

"I wanted to talk about how we fought off those dogs, then talk about fighting Thundersloth and how Calypso made friends with him."

"Nah, it went well. The man coming to get her kept you from saying too much," Juan Manuel assures his friend. "You want to leave her curious and if you *really* like her, you want to let them talk more, which is a good way to see if she's fun or if she'll drive you nuts." He pauses for a moment, then starts back up when he sees that he's gotten Good Boy's attention.

"Sometimes, they go hand-in-hand, but such is love! The trick is that you have to actually listen, not just sit there like it's something to get through. If you feel that way, move on. When you do talk, you definitely don't want to brag, it looks desperate and sounds like it might not be true. It wouldn't have made a difference to tell her that stuff if you never see her again and, if you do, you'll have another chance to show her rather than tell. Anyone can say anything, but bravery and strength come from within and that has to be shown. Some are so strong and brave that it can be seen in the way they walk."

Good Boy growls from frustration. "That sounds right. How do you know all this?"

"By making lots of mistakes. Even some of the times it went well, I was never sure if I was just having a good day or met a weirdo who likes awkward goats."

Good Boy laughs. "I haven't had the chance to do the same. With the number of female dogs I meet, I can't make too many mistakes."

"That's why I'm helping," Juan Manuel nods. "Trying to, anyway."

"You implying I'm hopeless?"

"No," Juan Manuel says, laughing a little. "More that I might be fooling myself by thinking that I know anything! And I'm really not sure how well my advice works with dogs. Hopefully it's kind of the same. I don't think anyone of any creature likes the mean or the cowardly unless they're the same way and, even then!" Juan Manuel says. "Sure, some settle or are fooled by bluster, but to someone who knows better, bragging makes one sound suspiciously like they're weak or mean."

Calypso scratches the top of her head. "Do you think that maybe they're mean because nobody really wants to be with them, just the fake version of themselves?"

"Maybe."

"I think the mean and the weak are one in the same," Good Boy says, his eyes on Zonda's handler across the parking area watching the restaurant Shriya and Miguel went into as he walks Zonda around.

"How so?" Juan Manuel asks.

"I think that maybe they're mean *because* they're weak. You know, so nobody messes with them, because if they did, it would reveal what kind of cowards they really are."

Calypso nods. "So the ones that sound the toughest are the weakest?"

"I don't know about *always* and there are different ways to be weak," Good Boy says. "There are some dogs that might do the tough-talking thing that you don't want to mess with because they can *really* fight, but they probably feel weak in some other way."

"Like how?" Calypso, asks, beginning to get distracted by hunger.

"One way could be that they feel lonely a lot because nobody wants anything to do with them. Maybe their person treats them bad and that makes them feel weak and worthless."

"But, why would they act tough if it makes the other dogs like them even less?"

"I don't know." Good Boy says, scratching behind his ear. "It could be they can't think of anything else to try."

"Ah, so they're also dumb," Calypso nods. "That's a sad combination."

"I think it's because they can tell themselves that the other dogs don't like them because they fear them rather than being disliked for who they are. With the first way, they get to feel like it's because they're better than them," Good Boy says. "Instilling fear could mean they're tough, which puts them higher in the pack, remember? With the second way, they have to face the truth that they were rejected because they're actually bottom of the pack. I hear with some groups of animals, it's loneliest at the top and the bottom, but being lonely at the top is definitely preferable to being lonely at the bottom." Zonda and her handler are finally getting ready to leave.

"OK, but acting tough isn't mean. Why are they mean?" Calypso asks.

"Because lying to themselves doesn't work really well, but treating others badly makes them feel like they really are higher in the pack. Of course, that's only when they get away with it. Every once in a while, they meet someone who actually is tough and they end up having a bad day."

Calypso shakes her head. "This is too complicated. Group animals are weird."

"Yeah, I sometimes think sloths have things figured out much better than us," Good Boy says, following Zonda's small truck leaving the parking lot with his head.

"Only *some*times?"

"Yeah," Juan Manuel says, "other times, there's nothing like the love of your group."

"Unless you're mean and nobody likes you," Calypso says.

"Right."

Calypso scratches her other arm. "Maybe if it feels so good to be loved by your group, it hurts just as bad when they don't love you?"

"I was always well liked, so I couldn't say," Juan Manuel shakes his head slightly.

"Because you were never mean."

"Well, I try not to be—there's no sense in it. You get more from being nice than being mean and, when someone helps you when you're nice, it's because they *want* to help, not because they're afraid of what you'll do to them if they don't. But that's not the biggest reason not to be mean. When I was a kid, I used to pick on this other goat. Nobody else much liked him, either, but I still feel bad I did that. At the time, I thought it helped me fit in and made me more liked. Now I know I just looked like a lower middle herder at best and I don't like that I was ever that kind of goat."

"You're definitely not like that anymore."

53

"I try to be the best goat I can be. I'm slowly getting there."

"You must have really high goals, then."

Juan Manuel tilts his head, "Nah, not really."

"Do you think I have that walk?" Good Boy asks Juan Manuel.

"What's that?"

"The walk of the strong and brave."

"Wow, you were really listening to me, huh? That or just can't get Zonda out of your mind. Well, yeah. I mean, you have this kind of fog of sadness or anger or something around you that probably doesn't work to your benefit, but nobody is going to take you for an ornamental dog or one of those that are all bark until the gate they were behind is opened and they run away."

"I did that very thing when they killed Pablo." Good Boy says looking into the distance.

"Nope," Calypso says, "he told you to get me and you came and got me. They were people with guns, they'd have killed all of us."

"Yeah, it doesn't count when it's people with guns," Juan Manuel says, nudging Good Boy's chin with his nose.

"Yeah, OK. All right, so how do I get rid of that fog?"

"I don't know. I don't have it, do I?" Juan Manuel asks.

"I don't think so."

"No," Calypso says.

"But you agree with him that I do?" Good Boy asks.

"Yes."

"It's because of what happened to Pablo."

"Yes," Calypso affirms, "It's been there since then. You might not have been able to save him, but you saved me."

"I know."

"Then why do you still feel bad?"

"I don't know."

"And you saved me after," Juan Manuel adds.

"OK, I know that if I didn't leave Pablo to get Calypso we'd all be dead, but you're both telling me I still have this fog."

"It's just a bad thing that happened and you can't change it, so you have to continue on with that as a lesson, not a way to punish yourself," Juan Manuel says.

"I know, but why can't I do that? Calypso has moved on from her mother and Pablo, and you from your herd and almost getting eaten."

"Eh, almost getting eaten wasn't a big deal," Juan Manuel says. "My whole herd died in a flood. It was only that I was able to get onto a tree that I survived. The people that found me decided to eat me. Honestly, after the flood killed everyone, I didn't really care that much if I was eaten."

"I didn't know," Good Boy says. "I've never heard you talk about that before."

"Why would I? Today is a different day and this is the one I'm living. Tomorrow, a flood might happen again and we could all die," Juan Manuel says, standing straight. "I want today to count and when I have to die, I want it to be with my head up high knowing I gave it all I had. Or in my sleep from old age with my grandkids playing around me."

"But, don't you see it over and over in your mind?" Good Boy asks.

"No, it feels so long ago that it might as well have been something that I watched from a distance. It's not something I think about." Juan Manuel pauses and looks at Good Boy, "Maybe it's because it happened so suddenly and fast that I didn't have time to notice anything to remember later. I heard a roar, some of the others called out in alarm, I saw all this mud and debris coming at us and my hooves came out from under me. Next thing I knew, I was being carried toward a tree and I was able to grab on. I don't remember seeing anyone else once the water hit."

"Maybe it's because it wasn't your fault," Good Boy says sadly, "like Pablo was with me."

"That doesn't sound like it was your fault, either. Flood water and people with guns are both nearly unstoppable forces."

Good Boy shakes his head. "It keeps going through my mind, the noise of the bad men approaching, seeing them through

55

the window, seeing them not even pause when I barked a warning and knowing that the time had come for me to die to save Pablo." A woman walking by does a double take at Calypso on Juan Manuel's back, stopping as if to pet her. Calypso lifts a hand full of claws at her and Good Boy barks a sharp warning followed by a toothy growl. "Sorry!" she says, backing away with a laugh. Good Boy blows his nose toward her as she walks away shaking her head.

Calypso reaches over and scratches Good Boy's head gently for several moments. "We're not a herd or a pack, but I guess you are my group, right?" Calypso asks.

"Of course. I don't know what they call a group of . . . us, but definitely." Juan Manuel says.

"How about a horde?" Good Boy suggests. "I saw on that tele thing, these great warriors that fired arrows from horseback were called a horde."

"I don't know," Calypso says. "I'm a sloth—should we be named after warriors?"

"You're a warrior." Good Boy insists.

"No I'm not!" she laughs.

"Of course you are. There's more than one way to fight."

"What type of fighting do I do?"

"You never give up," Good Boy tells her. "You could have gone up almost any tree at any time and lived your life, but you got us to safety time and again—"

"Untied me from the stake!" Juan Manuel interrupts.

"Yeah, you untied him, visited the land of the dead—"

"Mushroom!" Juan Manuel interrupts.

"Whatever it was, it was brave! You helped save the other two sloths, went up against a vicious chimpanzee in the tower, befriended Thundersloth and got him to help us," Good Boy lists off, his tail wagging slowly. "I'm sure I forgot some things, but the point is that you've never hesitated or questioned, you just did what you could and you never had to do any of it."

"How can you tell if a sloth hesitates?" Juan Manuel asks with a laugh.

Calypso frowns. "You saw me hesitate when you asked me to help rescue the annoying person in the chimpaneezee place."

"Hey, are we trying to save him again?" Juan Manuel snorts.

"What?" Good Boy asks, startled. "Are we?"

Juan Manuel shrugs his lip. "I don't know, that's why I'm asking. Calypso just made me remember that I heard Shriya and Miguel talking about Rondo."

Good Boy snorts derisively. "I hope not."

"What are we doing then?" Juan Manuel asks.

"Getting the boat back, I thought." Calypso says.

"I don't know why," Juan Manuel says. "Shriya has the other boat and that's the one she uses most. Are we getting it back for you?" he asks Calypso.

"Oh, I don't care about the boat." she says dismissively. "How do we tell Shriya so we can go home?"

"Right," Good Boy says. "You ever try to talk to her the way we do?"

"Yeah, but it's like trying to talk to a predator—they don't let you in." Juan Manuel says.

"Yeah, it never works for me, either," Good Boy nods.

"You ever try it?" Juan Manuel asks Calypso.

"No, I don't want to be in peoples' heads and I don't want them in mine."

"Not even Shriya?" Juan Manuel asks. "Isn't she in our group?"

"Yes. OK, Shriya would be fine, but if you can't get through to her, I don't think I can."

"How about we call ourselves a swarm?" Juan Manuel suggests. "Like in a swarm of bees. One bee be sting is mostly a nuisance, but together they're dangerous."

"That sounds more like people," Calypso says.

"I don't think there's anything that fits. Maybe we need a term of our own," Good Boy says.

"How about a *family*?" Calypso says.

Good Boy and Juan Manuel look at each other and nod.

```
         /\      /\
  _____ \ 0     0 / _____|||--/o) _ (o\--|||---------  ~ \  / ~
        \   \/  /                                         (      )  _____
          \/                                                \/
```

Miguel unties Buca and Juan Manuel while Shriya takes a look around to make sure nobody's watching before getting out a tourist guidebook and unfolding Rondo's letter hidden inside to check for the third time that the fake VINs match what she's entered into her GPS. Satisfied she didn't enter them incorrectly until the next time she questions herself, she notices the logo of the fake rental car agency at the top.

"You down with O-C-D?" Miguel asks.

"Huh?"

"You checking the numbers again? I was hoping you'd say, *yeah, you know me*, you know, from that '90s song?"

"Yup, I blew that one, but look!" Shriya points out the rental car agency logo.

"What about it?"

"I think he drew us a map of sorts."

"Are you sure?" Miguel asks. "It looks like a rock or something to me."

"Well, I think that's what it is—a drawing of a large rock or cliff face that I imagine must be what we're looking for."

"That's going to be tough to match up."

Shriya frowns, but agrees. "Yeah, probably."

"What if it's only some random scribble to look like a real business?"

"Not with Rondo."

"Maybe the motto is a clue?" Miguel asks. "*Cave RuinaS en Arcem*. Something about a ruined cave?"

"They're both clues," Shriya says. "*Cave* means *beware*."

Miguel gestures to the side of his head. "You speak Latin?"

"A little because of scientific names, but there was an old World War Two airfield my family used to ride our bikes by when I was young. The Americans had fighter planes there called a Thunderbolt and the motto was *Cave Tonitrum*, which means *Beware the Thunderbolt.*"

"You remember that?"

"Of course. My father was into it and would point it out every time we passed, but I like history, too."

Miguel leans in, "So, what does the rest mean?"

"Beware . . . something . . . ruins. Arcem . . ." Shriya traces her finger along the page, "I feel like I should know this one."

"Fortress!" Miguel exclaims, showing her the translation from his phone. "Look at that—who needs to learn Latin, anyway?"

"*Beware the fortress ruins,*" Shriya frowns. "We already pretty much knew it was an old fort. Not as helpful as I was thinking it might be."

"*Rondo* wasn't as helpful as I thought he'd be."

"Yeah, that's kind of a character trait," Shriya says, laughing, "but he comes through when something's important."

"So he must have discovered that it's the ruined fortress from the stories."

"Must be," Shriya agrees. "Not sure what to beware of, but I guess he could only put so much in here without it being an obvious code in case it was intercepted."

"I wonder if it's booby trapped."

Shriya shakes her head. "It's amazing that you can ask that question and it's completely reasonable."

"Yeah," Miguel agrees, "sometimes it's like we lived in an adventure movie nobody would believe."

"And now we're living the bad sequel." Shriya turns to Buca, Charleston, and Calypso. "Everyone ready? Let's go."

"See?" Juan Manuel asserts, following Shriya. "We *are* looking for Rondo."

Good Boy groans.

Calypso scratches her forehead. "I'd rather we were looking for the boat."

"I thought you didn't care about the boat?" Juan Manuel says.

"I don't, but I don't want to have been traveling all over the place just to end up with Rondo."

Good Boy stops short. "You don't think he'd move in with us, do you?"

"If he does, I'm staying with the goats," Juan Manuel says.

Calypso nods. "And I'm sticking to the trees where I belong, anyway."

"If he comes to live with us, *I'll* stay with the goats!" Good Boy growls.

"You don't want to live in the trees with me?" Calypso teases him.

"Too many monkeys."

"Not if you eat them."

"Why don't you move into a tree near the goats?" Good Boy teases her back.

"Are there good trees there?"

"Great trees!"

"Sure."

Cleaned and packed up, they all head to the car. Taped to the driver's window is a piece of paper with a picture of a man's face that looks as if it were printed on an old inkjet printer with a spitting cartridge and then photocopied on a machine that had been temporarily resurrected after being found in a dump before being sent through a fax machine. Over the man's eyes are black spots drawn in marker.

"Is that a picture of a human, or is it one of those lab chimps looking for a missing friend?" Miguel asks.

"Guessing from the context, I think it's Rondo," Shriya says, "Must be from our visitor last night."

60

"Is he supposed to be a blind pirate with two eyepatches?"

"Maybe they blinded him or killed him? Or maybe they're warning us they will?"

"Why stick that on the car?" Miguel looks around, but there are only a couple small groups of oblivious-looking regular people in sight.

"I would guess that it's a warning," Shriya says.

"But it doesn't say anything."

"Maybe vagueness is the point."

"To get us to stand here long enough trying to figure out what it means that they'll be able to escape with the treasure?" Miguel asks.

"I think the not knowing part is scarier than a specific threat."

"Or they were afraid we'd go to the authorities if it was specific? Whatever it means, I guess we didn't lose those guys after all."

"And they're showing they can get to us," Shriya adds.

"Except when they're scared off by a dog," Miguel says, patting Good Boy on the head.

"I think they just didn't want to take the chance of raising a ruckus—they can get to us any time they want."

"Do you think Rondo's dead?"

"If he isn't now, he probably will be," Shriya says. "Maybe we should go to the police."

"What can they do? Who do they even go after?" Miguel says. "Even if we tell them your theory about the coordinates, they would think we're crazy. Not that I don't want to, I just want to make sure they will help."

Shriya nods, looking around and wondering if there are eyes watching them. Seeing nobody, she gets in the car. Miguel walks around and opens the back door for the animals and gets in on the passenger side.

"What's going on?" Calypso asks Good Boy.

"I don't know. I think the man from last night must have put that paper on the car."

"They don't like it?"

"No."

"You couldn't have caught him, huh?"

"He was out of sight before we were out the door, then he got away in a car."

Calypso looks at Miguel and Shriya for a moment and blinks. "If the people are afraid, I don't like it."

"Neither do I."

"Me, neither," Juan Manuel adds.

"And all this for Rondo," Good Boy says.

Nightmare of the Crescent Moon

"We've reached the end of the road," Miguel says ominously as the dirt road shrinks to a path leading into the rainforest. The path is barely wide enough for the car to fit.

"Let's hope not." Shriya backs up and parks behind a small off-road vehicle with heavily weathered paint not much different from the patchy, peeling clear coat on her own car. "I'd try to continue up the trail, but if this off-road truck parked here, it's not a good sign."

"Yeah, if it gets narrower, the plants will scratch up your paint and think of what that will do to your resale value!"

"I'll have you know that this is the finest banger you'll find outside of a scrapyard."

Miguel pats the dashboard. "It does run well. Somehow." He nods at the off-road vehicle. "You think that could be another treasure hunter?"

Shriya opens the door and dons her boonie hat. "Sure, they're following the treasure map placemat they give to the kids at Capitán del Mar seafood restaurant."

Shriya and Miguel open the back doors and Buca, Charleston, and Calypso climb out. Shriya takes her backpack out of the trunk and hands Miguel's bag and rifle to him. They then go to take a look at the truck and feel reassured that it looks to have been sitting for a little while.

"I wonder if we could run into Zonda out here," Good Boy wonders aloud.

"I think we're really far from the . . . the place we were," Calypso says.

"But, I think that's the same car they were in," Good Boy says.

"How can you tell?"

"By the look of it!"

"They all look like that!"

"Not all of them." Good Boy nods to Shriya's car, "This one doesn't look like that one."

"OK, so half of them look like that and the other half look like this."

"What about Miguel's truck?" Juan Manuel asks. "That has the back part open to the sky."

"Do you see how many cars there are?—it's beyond counting!" Calypso feels Good Boy sigh in disappointment. "But, of course it could be the same," she tries to reassure him.

Good Boy, with Calypso on his back, sniffs the off-road truck and picks up Zonda's scent, confirming it's the right one, but doesn't bother to mention it. Juan Manuel locates and munches some vegetation—including one that is a mild pain reliever—growing alongside the edge of the road. A little more of that one . . . he smells goats. Other goats have been here. He looks up to see everyone at the forest entrance staring at him to follow. With some annoyance, he heads out after them.

Monkeys. They yell warnings to each other and occasionally throw things at the friends from the trees. With her sunglasses on, Calypso can barely make out their fast movements as blurs within the trees, and she wonders if there is any place safe from them. A piece of rotted fruit hits Miguel in the shoulder and he swings the rifle in the direction it came from.

"It's just a monkey, Miguel!" Shriya says, laughing.

Good Boy frowns when Miguel lowers the gun.

"It's funny when it's not you!" he complains to Shriya, wiping off his shirt.

Calypso agrees, understanding what Miguel said, despite not knowing the exact meaning of all those words.

Miguel wipes his hands with dirt to remove the sticky fruit residue. "Now the bugs are going to be even more attracted to me."

"Don't worry," Shriya says, spraying some extra bug repellent on him. "They prefer me, anyway."

Calypso reaches over and pats Miguel's leg gently in sympathy.

He looks down at her and scratches the top of her head, "Thank you, Calypso. See? She gets it."

"She isn't swinging a gun around."

Only because she can't, Good Boy thinks.

"Plus, she lives in the trees with them," Shriya continues, "so I'm sure she has more reason to dislike them than you do. Let's keep going."

"I wasn't actually going to shoot it," Miguel says. "I just wanted to feel like I could."

"Feel better?"

"Not with you giving me grief over it."

"I'm giving you grief because the seductive power of guns is dangerous."

"They're a useful tool."

"Yes, and like a chainsaw, there's a right way and a wrong way to use them."

"You're being ridiculous," Miguel defends himself. "It's not like I'm an American going around shooting everyone because they had some bad days."

"No, but it's a dangerous path to go down when pulling a gun is your first reaction to a minor annoyance."

"Fine, you are always right!"

"It's too hot to argue, Miguel."

"Who's arguing? You win."

"What are they arguing about this time?" Calypso asks Juan Manuel.

"I think Shriya didn't want him to shoot the monkey."

"Why not?"

"She likes them, I guess."

Calypso blinks with a slow shake of the head. "I thought she had better sense than that."

"If she had better sense, Miguel wouldn't be here," Good Boy says.

"I thought you didn't like monkeys, either," Calypso says.

"It's not about monkeys, it's about him not liking Miguel," Juan Manuel says.

65

"Because he's dumb," Good Boy says.

"Because Shriya spends time with him," Juan Manuel says.

"Yes," Good Boy agrees, "and that bothers me because he's dumb and she isn't."

"He bandaged up my horn and stopped the bleeding. He's not dumb," Juan Manuel says.

"He knows goats, but he's not as smart as Shriya."

"Well, no, but he's smarter than me!"

"He's a person, so dumb or not, he's still smarter than all of us," Calypso says to end the argument—everyone is being too noisy!

"Not all of us together!" Good Boy says.

"Of course he is!" Calypso insists. "Can we drive a car? Feed the boat the smelly juice? Work a gun?"

"No, but we probably could if we had their hands," Juan Manuel says.

"Those are pretty useful," Calypso agrees. "At least you have horns."

Juan Manuel frowns. "I have *a* horn."

"You're only missing part of one." Calypso leans off of Good Boy's back to get her nose closer. "I think it's healing well. It might even be starting to grow back," she lies with a nod.

"It is? How can you tell with the bandage? What do you think?" Juan Manuel asks Good Boy, turning his head down for him to smell.

"Oh, sure, it's coming along," Good Boy says, glancing up over his other shoulder at Calypso, who turns away to pretend to look at the trees.

"Ah, good, I don't want to look like those poor goats they take the horns off of."

"Well, you'd still have one," Good Boy says, "so that would depend on which side someone was looking at you from."

"Even so."

"Does it hurt?" Calypso asks.

"It's sore, but tolerable" Juan Manuel says. "I found some plants that help with pain, back near the car."

"That's good, but I meant about the goats that have their horns removed."

"I don't know, mine didn't get removed."

"But, you've talked to goats who don't have them, haven't you?"

"It's not really something we talk about."

"What do you talk about? Which plants are best?"

"Sometimes, but we talk about all kinds of things, the same way we do, but more goat-specific."

"What's goat-specific?" Calypso asks.

"I don't know, what do you talk about with the other sloths?"

"Sloths don't really talk to each other much. Once in a while, but we prefer to quietly stick to our own trees," Calypso says. "Except Drunk Monkey—he likes to talk a lot for a sloth." She scratches her head, "I guess I do, too, really, but only with you two."

"Swimming sloth doesn't like that name," Good Boy says.

"We all can swim, so that doesn't make sense as a name. He told me he liked it!"

"He told us he didn't when we called him that."

"Then why did he tell me that he liked it?"

"Are you asking why a male who really wants you to like him told you he likes the bad name you gave him instead of making you feel bad about it?" Juan Manuel asks.

"Yes."

"I just told you."

"No, you asked a question," Calypso says.

"The answer was in the question!" Juan Manuel blows a raspberry. Shriya glances at him, but keeps walking. "He wants you to like him, so he's saying he likes the name you gave him."

"He doesn't need to tolerate a name he hates for me to like him," Calypso says.

"Maybe not," Juan Manuel says, "but it's not unusual for any kind of male creature to do."

"OK," Calypso says. "I'll have to come up with a new name for him."

"I don't know how sloths work socially with not normally having names!" Juan Manuel says.

"I just said we're not very social."

"But, you are somewhat social."

"We know each other by smell, what's the need for names?"

"How do you talk to sloths about other sloths that aren't there?"

Calypso scratches her side. "Doesn't really come up. We don't talk about others."

"Then what do you talk about?"

"I'm trying to tell you we usually don't!"

"Not even to share crazy stories about what the dumb ones or the silly ones do?" Juan Manuel asks.

"We don't get up to crazy stuff," Calypso says, "and we don't know each other like that."

"I don't think I'll ever understand sloths. Hey, do you think people's hands grow back?"

"I wouldn't think so."

"Horns are better, then."

"Still on the horns!" Good Boy says with a head shake.

"She brought it up!"

Calypso blinks slowly. "Yes, that's my fault."

"Single-thought mind," Good Boy says.

Juan Manuel frowns and holds his head up. "Ah, feel that refreshing wind. I wonder if there's a name for that kind of wind."

"Yeah, farts," Good Boy says grumpily, frowning and letting one rip.

"Blah!" Calypso shakes her head. "I think he was making a joke about Zonda, because she's named after a wind."

"Yes, I know very well what he's doing," Good Boy growls softly

"So, you got him back," Calypso says, "but I have to smell it, too!"

"Sorry. Couldn't be helped."

Juan Manuel hops ahead and lets loose some of his own fermented emanation in response.

Calypso swipes the air in his direction. "Yech, stop it, both of you!"

Good Boy and Juan Manuel snort.

"They look like they're laughing," Shriya says to Miguel. "It's like Calypso somehow told a joke, except she looks distressed."

Miguel scrunches his face, "She is distressed! One of them farted."

"Oof, yeah," Shriya groans.

"Wouldn't it be amazing if animals found farts funny?"

"They might. Koko the gorilla made up scatological phrases all by herself to use as insults when she was angry," Shriya says, "showing that they have a similar outlook towards that kind of thing as we do."

"That's a gorilla, though. They're much more like us."

"Yes, but the more I study and observe animals, the more suspicious I am that the fundamental differences between all of us aren't as great as we like to think," Shriya says, glancing at Buca "Are we anthropomorphizing, or is that word used as an ignorant and arrogant, elitist dismissal by people too afraid or too insecure to open their minds?"

"I don't know, but I like my goats more than a lot of people," Miguel agrees. "Sometimes, they seem more human than people, you know?"

"That I do."

```
                /\        /\                                                      ~  \   /  ~
_____      \ 0    0 /      ---------|||--/o) _ (o\--|||---------      (       )    _____
                \    /                                                              \_/
                 \/
```

Almost an hour later, they all sit for a rest and some water.

Calypso wants to climb a tree, but Shriya pulls down some leaves for her to save them all the wait. It's not just about the food, it's about the trees! Still, Calypso appreciates the effort.

"How much farther is it?" Shriya asks Miguel.

Miguel pulls out his phone and checks the GPS. "Looking at how far we've gone so far, I'd say about another half hour, maybe more."

Good Boy hears something on the path ahead and stands up from his spot in the shade. A wide-shouldered person with a large, round head, flat face, and a boxer's nose comes around a bend up the hill, but it's the smell of Zonda and her handler that Good Boy recognizes, prompting him to stand straight and tall. Juan Manuel notices and steps up alongside him, in case there's trouble, but seeing Zonda, takes himself off alert and goes back to eating.

Good Boy barks a greeting and Zonda barks back. Shriya and Miguel stand as the man continues coming their way. Calypso climbs down Shriya and onto Juan Manuel's back.

"Didn't I see you back at the restaurant this morning?" the man greets the group.

"Maybe," Shriya says. "Was that your dog tied up to the fence out front?"

"Yes. Her name is Zonda."

"Cool name," Miguel says.

"What's his name?" the man asks.

"Bucephalus," Shriya says. "And the goat is Charleston, and the sloth is Calypso."

"What is the sloth wearing?"

"Sunglasses."

"Why?"

"She likes them," Shriya says. "I think they help her see better in bright light."

"Why do you have a sloth with you?"

"It's a long story. I found them as friends."

"You found them?" the man asks, letting Zonda off leash to sniff the edge of the trail leading her to Good Boy.

"It's more accurate to say they found me," Shriya says, "but yes, they were already friends. They seem to have decided to live with me."

"So, the sloth rides the goat, huh?"

"And Buca sometimes, too."

The man looks at the three animals thoughtfully for a moment, and then asks, "Did you find her with the glasses?"

"I did."

"That's amazing! So she must have been living with someone."

"Well, we can't see what it really looks like up in the trees. Maybe they have hardware stores up there."

The man smiles and offers his hand, "My name's Rico."

She shakes his hand, "I'm Shriya and this is Miguel." Miguel nods, but remains standing in the shade.

"Nice to meet you. What brings you all out here?"

"We're going to look for a paleotoca."

"A what?"

"It's a cave made by giant prehistoric animals," Shriya says. "I'm a paleontologist."

"I never heard of them."

"We're the people who study dinosaurs," she says dryly, knowing that he meant the paleotoca.

"I meant that I never heard of those caves." Rico says.

"I heard there was one up here. I'm skeptical, but it sounded worth a shot."

"So this cave was dug by dinosaurs?"

"Most likely giant ground sloths," Shriya says.

Rico nods at Calypso, who is still munching the leaves Shriya gave her. "You taking her to see where her ancestors lived?"

"Maybe."

71

"You expect some of them might not be extinct?" Rico asks, nodding towards Miguel's rifle.

"No," Miguel says, "but you never can tell what you'll run into."

Rico looks up the path and back at them, "There's a cave system up there that might be what you're looking for. I don't know what it looks like when a giant sloth has made it, but I can go with you."

"That's OK," Miguel says, "you can keep doing what you're doing."

Rico nods and smiles. "There's a goatherder up there. You could ask him to show you, too."

"What's his name?" Shriya asks. "In case we run into him."

"Rico. Same as mine."

"Interesting."

"It's a common name," he says. "Not too many Shriyas, though."

"There aren't many Ricos in India."

"Good point," Rico concedes. "Maybe we could use a few more Shriyas, and we can send some of our other Ricos to India. How did you get here?"

"By plane. I was going to swim it, but I was afraid of the sharks."

Rico grins. "I mean, you don't have an Indian accent and I was thinking it's odd that you ended up here."

"Well, imagine the most fantastic and wild story in your head and that will be a lot more interesting than the reality," Shriya says. "Leaving you with the better story will be my gift to you."

Rico nods, but his smile lives in the uncanny valley. "All right, then. Have a nice walk."

"You, too." Shriya says, a cagey smile of her own.

Rico walks off with Zonda glancing back at Good Boy who watches them until they get around another bend in the path.

Good Boy grumbles as they continue on their way, annoyed at not having much chance to talk to Zonda, and on heightened alert from the manner of the man with her.

"Something's not right about that guy," Miguel says.

"I don't trust him, either," Shriya says. "He was at the restaurant this morning, and I'm pretty sure that's a trained attack dog. What regular person would need a dog like that?"

"How can you tell?" Miguel asks. "A lot of people have scary dogs."

"The attitude," Shriya says. "She was calm, stoic, and evaluating us."

"Now that you mention it, Buca is more like that than most dogs."

"Dogs trained like that are specially selected and they're very expensive," Shriya says. "Unless he ended up with her the way I ended up with Buca, something's not right."

"I didn't notice any of that, but I got a bad feeling from him. That and his nose."

"Nose?"

"Either he's been in a lot of fights or he is into drugs. Looking at the size of him, it's probably not the drugs," Miguel says, consciously holding the rifle out in front of him before putting it over his shoulder.

"And I just thought he was unattractive." Shriya looks back to make sure they're not being followed, but doesn't see anything, and they continue on.

The rainforest starts to thin out and the path descends. "Do you smell the ocean, Miguel?" Shriya asks.

"I only smell myself!" Miguel says, sniffing his armpits. "I definitely can hear the waves." He stops and they all do the same. "Hear that? We must be getting close. I *hope* we're getting close."

"Asked and answered," Shriya says as the tree line ends at a cleared pasture area on their left. On their right, the land ends abruptly, the grass reaching over the edge of steep cliffs as if the blades are marching off the side to the ocean far below. The cliffs frame the bay in a half-moon shape with a central projection like a big-nosed man-in-the-moon. The jagged edges of the arms look to Shriya as if they repeat mathematically. "Fractals," she says out loud.

"What?"

"It's a geometric pattern that repeats in ever decreasing size."

"I understood every word you said," Miguel tells her, "but I have no idea what that means."

"Think of a snowflake."

"I've never seen the snow."

"Never mind," Shriya says, "it's just a weird thing that came to mind."

"This place matches the coordinates. What's that down there?" Miguel asks, ducking down.

Shriya crouches and follows his nod to a floating platform anchored a little less than a hundred meters from shore, surrounded by the cliffs that encircle the harbor. Another few hundred meters at the harbor entrance, a sleek sailboat with a bronze-colored hull and teak decks either still new enough to be golden brown or made of synthetic material rolls gently in the water.

Shriya takes out her binoculars, slides her hat off, and crawls to the cliff edge at the far end of the harbor opening. She shades the lenses from above with her hand to reduce the chance of a reflection that could give them away and trains them on the platform. Tied to it is a pram bow utility boat of about seven meters, with low freeboard and an outboard motor that looks bigger than it needs to be. There are several men just hanging around. Crates, air tanks, and equipment she can't identify are stacked in various places around the platform. Swinging the binoculars to the sailboat, she can't see anyone aboard, but it's even nicer than she had initially thought.

Miguel crawls up next to her. "See anything?"

"Not really. That sloop is a dream, though!" Shriya says. "It's very modern looking, but it has teak decking, which I love. Unless it's synthetic . . . I can't tell. Nice either way."

"It *does* look good."

"It also doesn't get slippery when it's wet."

"Practical and beautiful. No wonder you like it."

Shriya shakes her head with a smile.

"Looks like a good size," Miguel says "About fifteen, sixteen meters?"

"That's about what I'd say, yeah. Nobody moving that I can see."

"So we don't know if it might be the bad guys."

"Well, there's a platform and this is where we thought we needed to go," Shriya tells him, "so I say we treat them as if they are and they confirm we're in the right place."

Miguel crawls away from the edge and crouches out of sight of anyone below to survey the area. "This must be the fort."

Shriya crawls back and crouches next to him, seeing the sparse overgrown remnants of stone walls and raised ground of earthen embankments. She raises the binoculars to her eyes. The flat top of the middle of the cliff to their left is interrupted by conspicuously squared off raised pieces at almost regular intervals.

"It looks like what's left of a short wall with what could have been holes for cannons," she says, walking toward the far end of the cliff, but still far enough from the edge to not be seen from below. She trains the binoculars to the rear of the harbor and pans across the entire cliff that can be seen from her vantagepoint. At what appears to be about halfway down its length, the opposite extension ends abruptly in a broken off avalanche path, covered in a cascade of vegetation.

"It looks like some of it must have collapsed into the sea like the old legend says," she says.

"If Rondo has the right place," Miguel says. "There might be a lot of other forgotten forts on the coast."

"True." Shriya hands over the binoculars so Miguel can see for himself. He takes them and she shields the lenses with her hand. "Watch out, the lenses could reflect the sunlight!"

Miguel nods and puts his hand in place of hers. "We're too far back for them to see."

"Yes, I was making sure you knew."

He lowers the binoculars with a sigh. "Where do we start to look?"

Shriya is already looking at the drawing of the fake rental agency logo that Rondo sent them and trying to match it to the geography. To answer, she raises the paper.

"You find a match?" Miguel asks.

"Not from here. I think I need to get closer to the edge."

"I know that side is the collapsed side, but what if the drawing is for something on this side?"

"Yeah . . . if this tiny drawing is even accurate enough to know." Shriya stares at the cliffs as if they might reveal their secret if she looks at them hard enough. They don't, so she looks at the logo again, wipes some sweat off her brow, and turns the paper toward Miguel.

He shakes his head and pushes it back to her. "You're smarter than me and you know Rondo a lot better than I do," he says. "You might have better luck asking the animals."

"No, look at the motto. What do you see?"

"Latin. I thought you already translated it."

"Yeah, but is there anything odd about how it's written?"

He takes the paper and looks closer at it. "The *S* in *ruinas* looks like it might be capitalized?"

"OK, then that makes two of us," Shriya says. "I could ask the animals, but I think that's good enough."

"Do you think it's a direction? I know the small and the capital S look the same, but it's not even that much bigger."

"I think that's what it is. Rondo would realize that this drawing would only make sense from a certain perspective and I'm sure he thought I'd be able to figure this out."

76

"How well did you know this guy?" Miguel asks. "I don't even think a lot of married people would get these kinds of clues."

"When we first started to getting to know each other, we had a conversation about how the constellations only look that way from our perspective and he told me that, in high school," Shriya puts the paper back in her pack. "He tried to plot out some constellations from the perspective of one of the other known planets in a different solar system that could possibly support life."

"Let me guess, you were the first girl he dated."

"Haha, yeah," she says quietly.

"Did he figure any out?"

"He said he did a lot of research and math to get the relative distances to each other from that perspective, yet he ultimately figured he could never know if the stars he plotted would even form a kind of picture and constellations only loosely look like their stated resemblances in the first place. I think he thought it would impress me."

Miguel cocks one eyebrow. "That's an unusual pick up technique."

"I've heard worse."

"So, it actually worked because you're a super nerd?"

"No, I told him something like, even if he had figured out the whole night sky on the other planet, there would need to be intelligent beings with imagination there to observe them and there would be no way of knowing what they would relate them to in terms of what their world was like. He was trying to solve an unknowable philosophical question with a math solution."

"What did he say?"

"He agreed. He later told me that was when he had fallen for me," Shriya says. "The point is that the conversation was very important to him and he knows that I know that, so it makes sense that he would use the idea of perspective in a clue."

"You know what else it means?"

"What?"

"That he still loves you," Miguel says.

"I hope not!"

Miguel nods, not wanting to push the point. "OK, so do we face south or does the structure face south so that we should look north?"

"That I don't know," she admits. "Which way are we facing now?"

"North east?" He takes out his phone and opens the compass app. "Look at that—north east!"

"You're good."

"We're on the east coast and the sea is to our right. I don't need any special skill to figure that out," Miguel concedes. "So, if we go to the other side and look back here, we might be able to match it and if we don't, we can assume this is the right side to look from."

"Or I'm completely wrong."

"You were right about the VINs being coordinates. We must at least be close after that guy attempted to break into our hotel room," Miguel says, "and the drawing that was left behind on the car."

"Yeah, the first could have just been a thief that Buca scared off, but the second one would be a strange coincidence."

"I'm sure you're right. You're always right."

"Don't start, Miguel."

"I'm not starting anything—smart women are sexy."

"I don't know if I'm smart enough to make up for sweating from a hike in this heat."

"Nah. I'm sure—"

A number of goats bleat behind them. Everyone turns at the sound and watches as a herd of large goats comes down the pasture that was once the drilling grounds of the fort. A tall man shepherds them along, and Good Boy steps next to Shriya, looking up at her to see if he should take this guy as a threat or not. With no sign of fear, he stands quietly, warily. Juan Manuel steps next to Good Boy and Calypso switches to Good Boy's back.

Good Boy figures she's climbing off of Juan Manuel so that he can greet the other goats, but he would prefer she stayed with him in case he has to maneuver to attack. Juan Manuel makes no move toward the herd.

"Don't you want to run up and see the other goats?" Good Boy asks.

"No, way," Juan Manuel says. "This is their territory."

"But you have horns and these don't."

"I have *one* good horn and a broken one, which might be worse than none."

"What about that island we were on with all the crazy sheep?" Good Boy says. "You weren't afraid of those goats."

"That was different. There were a lot less of them and they were smaller. Even so, they weren't friendly."

"Yeah," Good Boy agrees. "Neither were the sheep."

"No, but the problem with sheep is they choose someone to follow, then stop thinking for themselves. If they had been with us at that sacred tree, they probably would have followed the ram off of the cliff."

"I wonder what the woman thought about everything that happened after we got away."

"She probably never knew why we left."

"With the sheep being loose and some of them wet, do you think she might have figured out that we were chased out of there?" Good Boy wonders. "Plus the ram being missing. She must have known the sheep weren't right in the head when she kept finding them impaled on the fence after every staring night sky eye."

"Maybe she didn't think much about it at all," Juan Manuel says. "People miss the things that happen around them a lot."

"That's true, but I'm sure she was disappointed that we left."

Calypso scratches Good Boy's head. "I'm sure she was."

The shepherd sees the group and walks over. Shriya smiles and Miguel puts on a cheerful mask as he steps forward to greet him.

"How are you two doing?" the shepherd asks. His sharp-featured face is weather-beaten and his early graying hair and the lines projecting from the corners of his cavernous dark eyes make him look older than the shine in them would suggest, eyes almost entirely on Shriya.

"Good, and you?" Miguel asks loudly.

"Not bad. Nice day out. The goats think so, too."

"Ours seems to agree," Shriya says, looking at Juan Manuel, who is cautiously greeting the more open members of the herd who approach him for a sniff.

"Aye, what happened to his horn?"

"He had an accident with a tree."

"Did you have him looked at?"

"Yeah, he'll be OK."

"I hope so, he looks like a fine goat," the shepherd says, admiring Juan Manuel. "That is why all my goats' horns are removed when they are young."

"I got him when he was already grown."

"Oh, you can't do it that late. Some people think that it is mean to have them removed, but you can see the problems they can have getting caught. Sometimes they stab each other or their owners, too," the shepherd says making a comically pained face as he uses his thumb to mime being stabbed in the stomach. "When they are young, they heal quickly and they don't remember it."

The shepherd finally notices Calypso on Good Boy's back and furrows his forehead. "Is that a sloth riding your dog?"

Calypso gives him a long blink.

"Yes," Shriya says. "The three of them are friends somehow."

"Sloths live in trees!" the shepherd insists.

"Yes, and she comes down to see her friends all on her own."

"And ride on the dog's back? You didn't teach her to do this?"

80

"No, I don't know how she learned," Shriya says. "The three of them showed up like this on my property one day and decided to stay."

"I have never heard of anything like it. You would think it's something you'd only see on a kid's cartoon."

"Is this your land?" Miguel asks.

"No, I bring my goats here to graze and keep the place clear. This is what remains of an old fort that I try to keep up by having the goats keep the vegetation down. Nobody has seemed too interested in this place until recently. You're not with the people in the harbor?"

"No, we saw this trail and decided to go for a hike," Shriya answers.

"That's the path I try to keep open in case there's an emergency. There's a river behind where I live," he gestures beyond the back of the fort, "It's not very big, but the nearest bridge that can carry a vehicle is before the next town and it takes too long to get to in an emergency."

"It's a little overgrown for a car to fit."

"Yes, it grows more quickly than my goats can eat it, but if you do not care about keeping the car's paint, there is room."

"Who are the people in the harbor?" Shriya asks.

"I don't know, but they are up to something," the shepherd says, looking around. "One of them told me this morning that I had to stop coming out here."

"Are you going to call the police?" Miguel asks.

"What are they going to do?" the shepherd shrugs. "Even if they cared, I don't own this place."

"Tell them your suspicions." Miguel says.

"Suspicions of what?"

"They threatened you, didn't they?"

"Not in a way that cannot be interpreted as a helpful warning. They told me they're going to be using explosives soon to stabilize the cliff." The shepherd frowns to show his doubt about the men in the harbor, then smiles as he notices his flock have already accepted the visitors. "I suppose they have as much right to be here as I do. I can graze my goats in back until they leave. I don't know who they are, but they are dangerous kinds of men. I saw you and came over to tell you that you should probably not stay here long if you are not with them."

"We won't. What do you think they're up to?" Shriya asks.

"I don't know. This is not a good place to smuggle things. I think there might be something buried under the water. They have a floating platform that they are diving from."

"Maybe it's lost treasure," Miguel suggests with a laugh, earning him a disapproving look from Shriya.

The shepherd looks wary. "I don't know, but you should head back. There are better ruins to see." He smiles at Juan Manuel, mingling with his goats. "Look how they get along already! If you are interested in selling your goat, I will buy him from you."

"No, but thank you," Shriya says firmly. "These aren't just animals, they're my family and they are not for sale."

"I am sure that is true," the shepherd says, "but as you can see, goats like to be around other goats."

"I have goats of my own and he visits with me a lot," Miguel says. "I have a business clearing vegetation, too."

"The clearing and the path is a favor to this place and because they have to eat. I have mine for the wool and to make milk products. Some of the milk is bought by animal rescues for different baby animals, including orphaned sloths."

"That's sweet," Shriya smiles.

"Yes, it makes me happy." He looks to Miguel. "How is the clearing business?"

"I'm never going to have my own airplane," Miguel says, "but I eat and I enjoy the work."

"It is a good living even if, like you say, you are not rich," the shepherd says. "The goats are always entertaining. If I lived somewhere less remote, I would maybe do vegetation managing as part of the business. I am glad that he has your goats, because they need to be around each other."

"That might be true," Shriya says, "but he would never leave his friends."

"These three were all traveling alone?" the shepherd asks.

"Yes. Riding them as you can see them now."

He shakes his head in marvel. "They must have been traveling with someone before they came to you. I wonder what happened that they ended up alone?"

"I think about it all the time," Shriya answers quietly.

"A dog and a goat," the shepherd nods. "OK, but a sloth who rides them like they are horses? How does such a thing happen? When I think I know everything goats can do, they do something to surprise me, but this . . . I never could have imagined. Animals are amazing."

"They are," Shriya agrees.

"I got these goats after my wife died of cancer," the shepherd says sadly. "I don't think it's too much to say that they saved my life."

"I know what you mean," Miguel nods sympathetically.

Shriya frowns. "What kind of cancer did she have, if it's OK to ask?"

He points to his lower abdomen. "It started in her ovaries. In the end, it was everywhere."

"I'm very sorry," Shriya says. "What was her name?"

"Christina." The shepherd swallows hard. "Three years . . ." his eyes tear up, so he turns to the goats. One of the little ones jumps on the backs of several adults to get across the herd and it makes him smile. "Look at that little one! He always makes me laugh."

"What are they talking about?" Calypso asks Good Boy.

"The man with the goats said that his wife died and the goats saved his life somehow. I think she might have gotten shot in the stomach or something."

"Shot with a gun?" Calypso asks.

"Yes."

"I don't like those things. What's a wife?"

83

"It's a . . . you know how people find a mate for a long time?"

"They do?"

"Some of them do," Good Boy says.

Calypso narrows her eyes a little. "Does that mean we're stuck with Miguel?"

"Ah, so you don't like him, either!"

"No, he's OK. I would like it better if Shriya could find someone like the Man."

"I don't think there's anyone else like Pablo," Good Boy says quietly.

"Yes. I still think about him."

"Me, too. All the time."

"He was really nice."

"He was the best," Good Boy says.

"Shriya is very nice, too."

"She's the best, too."

"I think there can only be one best."

"Nope."

Calypso stares off at the blurry shapes of grazing goats and half-listens to the people saying things she doesn't understand more than a few words of. "Oh, so what is a wife? We got distracted."

"*You* did. I forgot."

"That's true. So, what is it?"

"It's a person's mate that they've been with for a long time or have mated with . . . I don't really know exactly, but I don't think all people mates are called a wife."

"So, is Miguel Shriya's wife? He's been around for a while."

"I don't think so."

"That sounds sad for the shepherd," Calypso says. "Sloths don't have wife-mates, but I would be sad forever if you or Juan Manuel died. Hey, you're a shepherd, too! Maybe you could show the person some things."

"Yeah, some shepherd," Good Boy says, "chased off a dock by sheep!"

Calypso lets out her silent laugh. "Maybe not the best shepherd, but the best dog."

"No, I think we saw the best dog earlier today."

"I'm sorry I said those stupid things back at that fence."

"It's OK," Good Boy says. "You're still the best sloth."

"What about Thundersloth?"

"He stinks way too bad. Oh, and he tried to kill us at first."

"He *does* stink," Calypso agrees, watching Juan Manuel pretend to be knocked down by the playful head butts of some small kids. "Juan Manuel is the best goat."

"That he is."

"I'm tired."

"Me, too. Let's lay down."

Good Boy and Calypso move into the shade of the trees at the edge of the forest and fall asleep. Not quite long enough to fall heavily to sleep, Good Boy's nose and tuned ears pick up someone heading their way, waking him up. He opens his eyes to see Shriya standing above them and he jerks his head up at her. Behind her, the shepherd is collecting his goats. Good Boy checks to make sure Juan Manuel isn't with them and isn't surprised to see him standing behind Miguel.

"Come on, Buca, we're heading back," Shriya says.

They head back down the path and out of sight of the grounds of the old fort, then stop for some water and snacks.

"How long should we wait for the goat herder to leave?" Miguel asks.

"I hope he'll be gone when we're done taking a break," Shriya says. "If we're going to be able to make any meaningful attempt to find anything before nightfall, we won't be able to wait all day."

Presidio de Santísima Trinidad

Miguel comes back from his reconnaissance waving his hat from the corner of the path, the sign that the fort is clear. The movement seems to attract a nuisance insect as he ducks and swats the air around him. Good Boy chuckles and Shriya hands a branch of leaves to Calypso to grasp so she can eat while riding Juan Manuel back to the grounds of the fort.

The wind has picked up. Birds glide in circles around the cliffs of the harbor, floating on the air that circulates within it before spilling over the top. Shriya and Miguel climb to the edge of the fort and look across at the other cliffs, comparing Rondo's drawing to the features.

"I'm not seeing anything, even trying to picture it from different angles," Shriya says.

Miguel squints into the distance and agrees. "I think we're going to have to try the other vantage points."

"We need a story in case we get confronted."

"What if it's someone who recognizes us, like those guys who stole the book?"

"Then it won't matter," Shriya says.

"OK," Miguel says, not happy about how fatalistic she sounds, "how about we say we're just looking at the fort?"

"We probably shouldn't want to look like we're trying to avoid being seen."

"So, we want them to see us?"

"No," Shriya says, "but we don't want to look like we're being sneaky."

"So, you want to try to keep out of sight, but if we're seen, we don't try to hide?"

"You've got it."

Miguel nods toward the animals. "What about them?"

"They'll be used to seeing goats, so Charleston won't be a problem and lots of people have dogs."

"Calypso, though?"

They both look at Calypso, who is casually scratching her head on Juan Manuel's back.

"Yeah, I don't know." Shriya shrugs, "From a distance, maybe she'll look like a baby goat on his back?"

They all stay away from the edge to avoid possible detection and make their way to the projecting cliff in the middle of the crescent, climbing over berms covered in vegetation kept short by the goats and the remains of stone walls not far under the top layer of soil preventing anything with deep roots from taking hold. They can't hear the sound of any bad guys coming from the harbor over the wind and crashing waves, so they assume they're still good.

"Do you know how far down it is?" Calypso asks Juan Manuel.

"About the height of a real tall tree, maybe two normal trees."

"Could you climb it?"

Juan Manuel walks to the edge and looks down. "I don't know."

Calypso leans over and sees gray blurs far below. "What's down there?" she asks.

"The cliffs are pretty sheer, but it looks like there's enough ledge that I could climb them. They look solid enough to hold me," Juan Manuel says. "There's some grasses on the larger ones and I think I see a bird nest. Yup, that's a bird nest. The first ledge is kind of far down, so I wouldn't want to try to jump it unless we were being chased by people with guns."

"Well, I'm not a goat, so I was asking more about what's moving down at the bottom, if they're what Shriya and Miguel were looking at."

"Oh," Juan Manuel says. "There are some boats. There's a big one of those boats with a tree growing out of it at the opening to the big water."

"Like on that tele thing!"

"Yes. There are some people on a flat boat about the size of the one you drive tied up to what's either a small land or some other kind of flat boat," Juan Manuel pauses for a moment, his eyes trained on the boat. "A person just popped up from the water and handed something to the other people on the land-boat. There's a beach around the bottom of the cliffs that looks like it's made of the kind of sand the boat would ride up on easily. And there's a fallen tree trunk along it—big one—and some large stones like the ones up here."

Good Boy steps up beside them. "What's down there?" he asks.

"Some people with some boats—" Juan Manuel's ears pick up some weird noises directed at them from Shriya. Turning around, she waves for them to go to her. "I think they want us away from the cliff," he tells Calypso and Good Boy.

"Are they afraid we'll fall like that weird ram?" Calypso asks.

"I don't know, but I definitely could climb these," Juan Manuel says.

"How about we go to Shriya in case it's something important," Good Boy suggests at the same time as Calypso.

As they travel along the perimeter of the fort, Miguel and Shriya crawl to the edge every once in a while to compare the features from their new perspective to the drawing, each time being disappointed with what they see. Juan Manuel and Calypso watch them disinterestedly and eat the vegetation at the edge of the forest that continues along the far side of the fort. So she doesn't have to climb, Juan Manuel stands up tall for Calypso to reach a lower branch of a small cecropia tree that has young leaves on it. They taste better when they grow from the tops of the large trees, but she doesn't want to be too far from the ground in case something happens.

The raised earth covering the ancient outer wall of the far side of the fort ends abruptly at the cliff's ragged edge, leaving nothing of the main wall that would have faced the sea. Hot and exhausted by the time they reach this unceremonious end, Shriya and Miguel sit to eat in the shadow of a small hill. Whether the entire hill is a natural feature utilized by the fort builders, or the result of hundreds of years of soil and vegetation collecting over smaller stone works, they don't know, but a thick growth of clinging vines can't completely hide a few remnants of stone near the bottom. Good Boy runs over to get some water and sit with them. He laps it up from a large water bottle held in Shriya's hand as she turns to Miguel with annoyance.

"I really don't think this is the time for that?"

"For what?" he asks.

"For fooling around w—" she suddenly notices that she can see both of his hands and leaps off the ground. A snake slithers out of a crevice in the wall between where two stones had separated, sticking its tongue out at her without concern. Miguel leaps up and raises the machete above his head. Shriya grabs his arm to stop him.

"Don't! It's a constrictor."

He lowers his arm. "Yeah, but he looks shifty!"

The snake disappears down a space between some vines. Shriya steps back, then throws her hat on the ground.

"Look!"

She traces her finger in the air to outline the faint shape of a stone cove in the vine-covered berm and holds Rondo's letter out to Miguel. "It's not the landform, it's this!"

"That's a pretty good match! But what does it mean?" Miguel asks. "If this is some kind of an entrance, nobody's been down there since Captain Morgan was around."

"Maybe the treasure is a stash of old rum." Shriya puts her finger on a couple of slices in the vines that look to have been cut by a machete.

"You think it could have been Rondo leaving a clue?"

"That or something happened and he stopped before someone figured it out." Shriya pulls out her own machete and the two of them hack at the vines along the sides of the cove to reveal the opening of a chamber.

89

Miguel takes out his phone, turns on the light, and shines it inside. "It's pretty open in here!"

"Yeah," she points at remnants of a rotted board sticking out of the dirt piled up behind the vines along the bottom of the entrance, and leans down to touch it. It's soft enough to crumble beneath her fingers. "I think someone might have boarded it up, then the vines grew in, and the soil packed up between it before the wood rotted away."

"But if this is the place, how would Rondo have known without having been in here?" Miguel asks.

"Maybe he found something that pointed him in this direction?"

Miguel puts his arm in front of Shriya to step in first and Good Boy steps up alongside her.

"Do we wait for Calypso and Charleston?" Miguel asks.

"No, leave them to eat," Shriya waves absently.

"That was a joke."

The thick roots give way to a large, humid space, cooler than outside and smelling of mold and earth. The light shines on the vaulted stones still holding fast against nature and gravity hundreds of years after their purpose was fulfilled. Most of the small pavers that had made up the floor appear to have been removed. Only a few remain to line the far left side of the chamber.

"What do you think this was?" Miguel asks.

"I don't know much about these things," Shriya says, "but I'd guess it could be a magazine."

"Seems located kind of close to the outer walls in case of a fight."

"Close to the cannons."

Miguel nods and looks outside. "Yeah, what's the elevation on a ship's guns? A ship might not even have been able to hit anything this high." His light lands on a small number of cannonballs half buried in soil against the far wall. "Did you guess it was a magazine or did you see these?"

90

Shriya looks in the direction he's facing. "Lucky guess." she says.

"No, it was a smart one."

She smiles politely and turns her light on the cannonballs. "I wish I knew more about this kind of thing so I could figure out what kind of guns they had here."

"Does it matter?"

"No, I'm just curious."

"Not very big ones, it looks like," Miguel says. "I thought the cannonballs would be the size of bowling balls."

"I suppose, it was a small fort in an odd place with a small field of fire. Have you ever seen candlepin bowling?"

"No," Miguel says, "what is that?"

"It's bowling with smaller balls and pins. We used to play it sometimes at uni. I'm not a bowling expert, but I think it's a Boston thing as I've never seen it anywhere else," Shriya explains. "Those cannonballs are about the size of candlepin balls. I wonder if this place was meant as a protected area for careening or emergency repair."

"Canteening? You mean, pick up water?" Miguel asks, mishearing her. "The shepherd said there's a river behind here."

"*Careening*," Shriya answers. "They would beach the ships and burn and scrape off all the marine growth from under the waterline and make any repairs. Obviously, they would be really vulnerable while this was going on."

"Wouldn't they do that in a port city?"

"I would think so, but I can't think of another reason for this weird, isolated concave fort."

Miguel turns his light down a hallway that once pointed to the ocean, but the ceiling at the end has since collapsed. In front of the pile of fallen ceiling stones, a large hole about wide enough for four people to stand alongside each other and almost high enough to stand up straight, leads down at an angle into the collapsed rubble. "What's this?" Miguel asks.

"Looks like someone dug it out." The tunnel reminds Shriya her of a dungeon.

"Yeah, but . . . Rondo? Could there be another way in here?"

"With an army doing the work, maybe," Shriya says wryly, "Rondo was never one for hard work."

Miguel inhales sharply and turns to her. "Maybe it was that guy who said he found the treasure!"

"Mr. Santiago," Shriya agrees. "I can't remember his first name. If the stories are true, that was about a hundred and fifty years ago."

"Only one way to find out." Miguel kneels down and shines the light into the hole, revealing thick cobwebs and hanging roots and moss like layers of curtains. He turns back to Shriya. "What's that old movie with the giant spiders called?"

"I don't think I saw that one."

"You want to go first this time?"

She grimaces at the webs. "Well, you're closer than me, so . . . don't set off any booby traps."

"What are the chances of that happening again?"

"I wouldn't take that bet."

Miguel takes a deep breath and ducks through under the top of the tunnel with Shriya right behind him.

Good Boy slips past both of them and descends what had once been stairs carved into the stone, but is now more like a ramp from the dirt that has washed down and largely filled in the space between the steps. Behind him, Miguel hacks and sweeps his way through the cobwebs, moss, and roots. Old bones—the smell compels Good Boy to stop and Miguel almost trips over him.

"What is it?"

Good Boy turns to him and barks. Miguel crouches down and shines the light as far ahead as he can get it. Almost hidden against the left wall by the hanging vegetation and the mud is a seated human skeleton, its arms fallen to its sides, left leg missing, and a twist of old roots leading up from its chest to a crack in the vaulted ceiling. More tendrils reach for, but don't quite touch the floor.

"I don't think it's Rondo," Miguel says," even bugs wouldn't like him enough to eat him that quickly."

"I don't know, if he still eats like he used to, the bugs might have gone crazy for the sugar and caffeine in him."

Miguel laughs and crouches down. "It almost looks like he was impaled by roots. Even I can't sit on the couch long enough for roots to grow into me."

"I don't think I've seen you sit for longer than two hours at a time," Shriya teases him. Inspecting the skeleton with her light, she looks through the rib cage and illuminates a sharpened stone about half a meter long and five centimeters square penetrating the sternum. A toughened root has wrapped around it so many times that it nearly forms a ball before several of them continue down to the dirt under the bones.

"Look!" she exclaims. "It looks like he was killed by this big stone, kind of like an axe, or a hammer with a wide chisel tip." She pries away some of the roots to shine the light inside, revealing a horizontal hole through the center of the stone with another near the back, and follows the roots up with her light to a stone tab protruding from the ceiling near a large crack where the roots grew in. Looking carefully around the tab, there's another one in parallel about five centimeters away. The tabs have holes drilled through them that line up with each other so that a rod could pass through them both. Tracing a path with her light straight down from the tabs, Shriya lands on the skeleton's stone.

"What do you think?" Miguel asks with a smile.

"A booby trap."

"See?"

She lets out a sharp laugh. "Most of it was probably made of wood that rotted away. I imagine there was some kind of an arm that the killing stone must have rode on." She turns her light to the ceiling again.

"Yeah, I see that," Miguel says. "It must have pivoted from those tabs.".

"The roots must have grown in before the arm completely rotted away and then they climbed down it to eventually reach the dirt." Shriya scans the ceiling, walls, and floor, but doesn't spot anything obvious. "Whatever triggered it is probably either long gone or buried in the mud."

"Pretty good," Miguel compliments her.

"I'm used to trying to recreate lost moments in time," she deflects. "A hundred-fifty years ago? Pffft! I work with animals that died tens or hundreds of thousands of years ago."

"I wonder who this was. Maybe it was the guy who dug this and accidentally set off his own trap."

"Maybe," Shriya says, "but it sounds like a lot of people tried to find this place back then."

"I guess with the traps made of wood, they might have only been working for a few years before rotting away." Miguel is silent for a moment. "Well, we should probably be careful in case there's a working trap that we can't see." He hacks down one of the thick roots and finds it sufficiently stiff, if a little heavy to hold stretched out, so he uses both hands to extend it ahead of them.

"This time, the root can go first," he says, and they continue down the crude stairs with Miguel hitting all sides of the passage with the root in the hopes of safely triggering any remaining traps that might be made out of more durable materials that could still function.

There aren't any more skeletons in the tunnel and the people don't seem too concerned about the first one, so Good Boy has no idea why they're continuing to the bottom where it just ends, but he's fascinated by the interesting smells of moss, mold, and decaying vegetation in the damp air. Miguel grabs his collar and tugs on it to stop him from getting ahead.

Good Boy looks up at Miguel in annoyance, then figures there must be a reason, so he leaves him to head the charge. Miguel immediately slips onto his side and slides down the rest of the dirty slope, the beam of his light bouncing off the walls and ceiling in a disorienting pattern until he comes to a stop some way down.

"Miguel!" Shriya yells out.

"Oof! I found the end!"

"Are you OK?"

"I don't think the stains will come out of these clothes."

"They're not blood stains, are they?"

Miguel stands up and checks himself. "Nah . . . maybe a little. Only some scrapes. Good news is there don't seem to be any live traps!" He shines his light on the stone that stopped his travel.

Shriya and Good Boy half-slide their way down the stairs to get to him.

"You're sure you're OK?" she asks, shining the light over his filthy clothes.

"Yeah, I'm fine."

She checks him closely with the light, then nods and turns her attention to the end of the passage. "You've got to be kidding me. This is it? Why did he build an armed trap before he finished the tunnel?"

"Do you think this could be a trap boulder with some kind of secret lever or loose stone or something that we have to move to release it?"

"If it *is* a trap," Shriya says, annoyed, "I doubt it's a resettable kind. We could try digging up some of this mud piled up around the bottom, but I don't see anything else." She shines her light around the edges of the wall, then takes out a folding knife, using the tip of the back side to clean out where the side walls and the end of the passage meet. "Hmm, yeah, there's a seam here."

"A deadfall trap." Miguel shines the light around the top to look for a gap, clearing some moss and roots out of the way. Sure enough, he finds a space big enough along the left side to stick his hand up to the wrist. He shines the light in the hole, but can't see how far it goes.

"See anything?" Shriya asks.

"No. Maybe it's a pocket where this stone came from. Well, all we need is some kind of drill that goes into stone and a hundred kilos of dynamite."

"I left that in my other pack back at the house."

"You can get that from your work, though, right?"

"What do you think I do at work?"

Manuel shrugs his shoulders. "Dig up old skeletons."

"They prefer we be a little more careful than that, but blasting would make it a lot quicker," Shriya says. "Of course, it might also collapse the whole tunnel—I've never blown anything up before."

"I've only blown up a couple of toilets after some bad food."

Shriya laughs and looks back up the tunnel where outside sunlight illuminates the outline of the hole in the collapsed ceiling near the top. Trying to get a better idea how far down they are, she shines the light up, but it's too weak to reach all the way. "How far down do you think we are?" she asks.

Miguel scratches his head and imitates the slope of the stairway with his hand. "I'm not sure how far down we are, but as I showed you, the slope is pretty steep."

"Yes, that was helpful, thank you," she smiles.

"My guess is that we're about two-thirds, three-quarters down the height of the cliff."

"You think the skeleton is about halfway up from here?"

"Maybe about that, why?"

"Probably means nothing and it doesn't help us either way," Shriya says, "but I'm wondering if whoever made this rigged the traps up evenly. It might be the one-third mark to the dead person and another third to this stone. Of course, even if we knew that he built traps at equal distances, they might be every quarter and we'd be only halfway down with another potential trap in between."

"Yeah, you're right."

"Well, it's only a wild guess."

"No, I mean you're right that it doesn't help us either way," Miguel says. "How do you think he figured all this out?"

"The dead treasure hunter, or Rondo?" Shriya asks. "Rondo's really smart."

"Rondo. He obviously never made it down here, but he was sure enough about this place to send you the clue in a code."

"True."

"And I don't see another way he could have gotten into the room upstairs."

"OK," Shriya says, looking him dead in the face, "what are you thinking?"

"I don't know, I . . ." Miguel shrugs and looks around. "He wouldn't know this was blocked off and that we couldn't get to the treasure. What if someone's betrayed him and he was able to send the clues to you so you could get the treasure and trade it for his life?"

"That's possible," Shriya agrees, "but I don't know if he'd intentionally send me into danger."

"Even if his life was on the line?"

She rolls the question around in her head a little. "Maybe. Or maybe he's dead." They are both quiet as that possibility sinks in.

"Since we can't get whatever treasure might be at the end of the tunnel with this boulder in the way," Miguel says, breaking the silence, "we should probably contact the police."

Good Boy thinks he hears Juan Manuel and turns his ears to the top of the slope. Human footsteps. His warning bark echoes painfully off the walls and the people go quiet and look up the ramp. Shriya pulls the rifle from the back of Miguel's pack, gets down on one knee against the wall, and aims for the outside light at the top. Miguel swings his pack around in front of him and presses himself into an indentation in the opposite wall. Good Boy leans against Shriya as a shield, the people kill their lights, and they all wait.

"I know you're down there," a man calls from the top of the tunnel. His voice sounds like Rico, "Zonda tracked you and I heard your dog barking."

"What do you want?" Shriya shouts.

"The same thing you do—the treasure of the Santa Teresa!"

"We're looking for Rondo."

"Did you find him?" Rico asks.

"Come on in and we'll talk," she says.

"My silhouette against the entry would make for an easy shot, wouldn't it?" Rico laughs. "Why don't you come up here?"

"It's nice and cool down here."

"Come on, now. It's not just me up here—there are far more of us than there are of you."

"You can only fit one at a time through the narrow doorway," Shriya challenges. "We've got plenty of ammo and it wouldn't be the first time we had to use that tactic."

Miguel nods in the dark and whispers, "That was badass!"

"I think we can wait you out," Rico menaces them. "Now that you've found the entrance to Santiago's tunnel, I could seal you in here and come back when you're dead." There is an ominous silence, and then he continues. "You know, I bet my friend Correa, there was no tunnel and that we'd have to blast everything underwater. Damn, now I owe him some money."

"There's nothing down here but a dead end and a skeleton that could very well be Ramon," Shriya tells him.

"Sure there isn't."

"Come down and see. Either Ramon didn't find the treasure or it's already gone."

"Oh, it's not gone, but we've been looking for the possible tunnel to get to the bulk of it for weeks . . . thank you!" Rico chuckles. "We were looking along the base of the cliffs. It seems obvious that it would be up here now that I know where it is. Quite the feat to tunnel so far in those olden days. Impressive!"

"I'm telling you there's no treasure down here!" Shriya insists.

98

"Too bad for you that I don't believe you."

"All of you morons couldn't find this place and we just happened to stumble on it without even trying, but you're going to trust what you believe over my word?"

"You know, it's funny how small the world is," Rico says. "Our old friend Pablo Rios had discovered this Spanish treasure while picking up a shipment of weapons and we wanted to help him retrieve it, but he decided he didn't want any help. We figured he might have written the location of where he found it and left it on his boat, so we run out to it and the boat runs away in front of us. Do you want to know who took the boat?" There are some clunking noises coming from the top of the tunnel and Shriya wonders what Rico is doing up there. "You already know, don't you?"

"That dog and the sloth!" Rico finally says after getting no response. "Then the boat shows up again at the dock in our town and the sloth and the dog come to the general store to steal dog food. Then they come back later and free a goat we were going to eat, knock a guard we set up at the boat into the water, and they all get away from us again!"

"If you're trying to argue that you're not a bunch of wankers, this story isn't helping your case!" Shriya shouts.

The man takes a moment to respond, breathing heavily enough to hear it in his voice, "Of course, by then, we had searched the boat and didn't find anything—not even the ledger he used to write down the coordinates of his pickup sites—so we concluded that Pablo must have kept the ledger somewhere secret if he wrote the treasure location anywhere at all, but whatever might have happened, the treasure was lost to us and it's a story we tell sometimes about the genius animals. One of us thinks they are agents of the Devil!" The sound of a match and a moment later, a cloud of exhaled cigarette smoke interrupt Rico's monologue. Good Boy barks his disapproval.

"*Then* not too long ago," Rico continues, "a man comes to Salvador looking for some quiet help retrieving a lost treasure he knows the location of, but lacks the ability to recover. We play nice, we play *not* nice, and he still won't tell us where it is, but before he fully understands the situation, he tells us about an old girlfriend who had been with him when he found the clues to the treasure in a pyramid in the jungle—an Indian paleontologist." Rico pauses again and coughs.

"Classically beautiful, elegant, he said, but he won't give us a name. Not even after we remove a finger."

Shriya's blood runs cold and she sees Miguel turn to her out of the corner of her eye, but she holds the rifle steady.

Rico continues, "Maybe he would talk if we put him through an even more extreme weight loss program, maybe not, but we realize we have enough to find you." More clunking and some pounding of stone. "And do you know what else we find when we find you? Pablo's boat! What is inside the boat this time? The ledger! Tell me, where did you find it?"

"Up your mother's ass!" Miguel shouts.

"Very clever, goat man," Rico sneers, his voice sounding a bit more distant and echoing. "You must be the amusement of all the school boys. Where was it, classically beautiful Shriya Deshpande, paleontologist?"

Shriya growls under her breath and Good Boy turns to her. "Hidden under a grate in the sole," she says.

"Ah, you know, I told Dom to look everywhere and I guess he didn't know what everywhere means. Thank you for finding that for us. It took a little while to figure out his code, but we found this place. Did you really come out here to rescue Rondo, or were you trying to beat us to the treasure?"

"Beat you *with* the treasure!" Miguel shouts.

"The adults are speaking, goat man!"

"I thought I'd use the treasure to secure his safety," Shriya says.

"What? Speak up!"

"I was going to use it like a ransom payment!"

"You would risk your life and give up a fortune for this annoying guy?" Rico scoffs. "Pssh, he did not deserve you!"

"Is he alive or not?" Shriya asks.

100

"He's alive for now, in case we still need him for something, though I can't imagine what, but your immediate concern should be for yourselves." Rico menaces. "It seems such a waste to seal you in here, but there are a lot of pretty women. As for you, goat man, even your goats won't miss you!"

The last ray of sunlight winks out as Rico clonks the final stone into place to seal up the entrance to the tunnel. "This is kind of becoming a theme for us," Miguel says, feeling his way closer to her.
"Yeah, and I don't like it."
"I don't think we'll get out the same way we did last time."
"I don't think we'll have to," Shriya says. "He couldn't have built anything too formidable, so we should be able to wait a short time for him to leave before digging our way out."
"Unless they're standing guard up there."

```
                                      ~ \   / ~
-------------|||--/o) _ (o\--|||--------  (     )  --------------
                                          \_/
```

From the safety of the higher branches Calypso had climbed to when Zonda and the other people showed up, she can barely make out Juan Manuel hiding behind some trees a short distance from the cave. Zonda paces and barks pleadingly at the people with her, making Calypso nervous. Three people are piling something, then hammering away on the pile for a while, before they walk away with Zonda, talking and laughing in a manner that Calypso doesn't like.
She decides to climb down and hear what Juan Manuel has to say about it. When she reaches the bottom of her tree, she sees Juan Manuel kicking at a wall sealing the entrance to the cave and she realizes those people had enclosed Good Boy,

Shriya, and Miguel inside. The wall seems to be reinforced by sticks jammed into the ground and angled at the stone blocks that had once been part of the fort.

She can hear Good Boy's muffled barks and Juan Manuel bleats back in a panic at the unmoving stones. Calypso scratches her head and calls out to Juan Manuel, who comes over to get her. Back at the cave, she can hear everyone on the other side trying to get through. Juan Manuel head butts the wall a few times, jolting her off him so that she has to climb back on. "Doesn't that hurt with your broken horn?" she asks.

"Yes. Any ideas?" he asks.

She looks at her claws and blinks at the rugged stones. "We need Thundersloth."

"All I can think of is to wait to see if the bad men come back, then we attack them."

"We?"

"OK, me."

"One goat against people and an attack dog?" Calypso asks. "We need a better plan."

"Not just me," Juan Manuel says. "Good Boy and the people once the bad person lets them out. I'll sneak attack from the side."

"Won't Zonda smell you?"

"This whole place smells like goat!"

"What if they don't come back to let them out?"

Juan Manuel makes a fart sound with his mouth. "Do you want to go back to the tree?"

"Yes. It will help me think."

"The stones seem like they've been wedged in really well," Shriya says, stepping away from the blocked entry, taking off her boonie hat, and wiping a dirty hand across her sweaty forehead.

"Maybe there's another weak point, like where the roots came in?" Miguel suggests. "I have a folding shovel on me."

102

"Let's give it a shot. If it causes the ceiling to collapse, it solves all our problems."

By the light of a phone, Miguel takes the shovel out of his pack, unfolds it, and tries to pry apart the blocks. The shovel tip pops out with a violent metallic clang.

Good Boy hears some noise from the blocked end of the tunnel and barks in that direction. Shriya shines a light, but doesn't see anything and turns back to Miguel. Good Boy barks again and looks back at them, but they aren't paying attention. Miguel works the end of the shovel into the crack again and tries to open it, but it pops out, sending some small chips and dirt flying onto his face. He curses and puts the shovel down to clear out his eyes.

Shriya puts her arm on his shoulder. "Maybe there's something that can re—"

Miguel puts a finger to her lips and points into the air.

Crunch! Some scraping sounds and another pinging crunch comes from the other side of the wall down by the boulder that blocks the lower passage.

Good Boy barks again in the direction of the noise, which changes to the heavy thud of solid steel and the sound of falling stones behind the wall.

Miguel takes a hold of the light and shines it toward the sound. "Are they trying to dig around the boulder?"

"I don't know. How would they even get this deep so fast?" Shriya asks as she swings the rifle into the dim circle of light at the end of the tunnel. Good Boy barks and she tells him to quiet down, but he doesn't listen. Miguel props up the phone to shine at the end of the tunnel ahead of them where it can't hurt their vision and takes cover behind Shriya, who is leaning against the wall behind the old bones, bracing the forestock on her knee and the stone sticking out of the skeleton's rib cage, aiming in the direction of the noise near the boulder at the end of the tunnel.

It's a long wait, sweat threatens her grip on the rifle, and her foot bent beneath her has fallen asleep, but a small sheet of stone has slipped from the wall and the pointed tip of a pickaxe appears, accompanied by some indistinct cursing of relief. Another whack and a bigger hole opens, displaced rocks knocking and rolling down the tunnel.

"Hello?" a voice calls in.

"Bahahahahaha," Juan Manuel bleats from a distance further back.

Good Boy barks excitedly and Shriya relaxes the gun and stretches her foot.

"Is that the shepherd?" Miguel whispers. He's partly drowned out by the pickaxe, but Shriya figures out what he asked.

"I think so. Sounds like Juan Manuel might be with him."

"Of course, who else?" Miguel says. "He must have gotten help!"

"We're here!" Shriya yells, shaking her leg out to stand on pins and needles as Miguel retrieves the phone. Good Boy barks and Juan Manuel calls back.

The shepherd's pick attacks the hole faster, rubble clunking and showering onto the floor of the tunnel. When it seems like it might be big enough to squeeze through, the shepherd sticks his head in, blinking at the shine from their light.

"Can you fit through?" he calls to them.

Miguel nods to Shriya, who cautiously half-slips down to the hole and Miguel stumbles behind, putting his leg out against the boulder to stop himself.

Shriya encourages Good Boy to go through the hole, but he's not sure if they can fit, so he won't leave them.

Shriya hands the rifle to Miguel and takes her pack off to hand it to the shepherd, who takes it and puts it aside, then she lifts Good Boy and tries to direct him through, but he pushes back with his paws, whining at her.

"Maybe you need to go first and he'll follow you," the shepherd suggest.

Shriya looks down at Good Boy with a frown and he looks back up at her. She smiles, pats his head, and lines herself up with the hole. The shepherd offers a hand to help her climb through. It's a tight squeeze, but she's able to kick and drag her way to the other side. She whistles and Good Boy looks at Miguel.

"Go on," he says, motioning to Good Boy to go first. With a groan of annoyance, Good Boy hops up and scrambles through. Next, Miguel pushes his pack through, then the rifle. Shriya takes them and puts them next to her smaller pack before helping Miguel. His shoulders catch on the sides, so he wiggles his way back into the tunnel.

"I should have tunneled up a little higher. Let me open this up more," the shepherd suggests.

"No, I can make it," Miguel says, "just help pull me through."

This time he goes through with one arm forward so he can angle his shoulders to reduce the clearance he needs. Shriya grabs his arm with both hands and braces her legs on the wall to pull as Miguel pushes off with his legs and with a scrape, some dust, and a tear from his shirt, he's able to get the top of his body past the hole and push the rest of himself into the rescue tunnel. He checks his shirt and sees the pocket dangling. He's also lost two buttons in the middle. He rips the rest of the pocket off. "I don't even know who actually uses these except for nerds in Hollywood movies. Anything you put in them falls out when you bend over."

"Thank you for getting us!" Shriya says to the dirt covered and sweaty shepherd. "I don't think we introduced ourselves last time. I'm Shriya and this is Miguel and Buca."

"Enrique."

"Don't think I'm only being polite when I say it's very good to have met you!"

Enrique smiles shyly at her.

"How did you know we were stuck in here?" Miguel asks him, looking around the tight confines and noticing that the tunnel branches off to continue downward around the boulder.

"And how did you get to us so fast?" Shriya asks.

"Let us walk and I tell you, we need to be away from here." Enrique leads them up a tight tunnel with a small lantern barely lighting the way. He talks as they stoop and climb their way along the stone and dirt walls.

"Your goat came to me so I followed to the remains of the fort. He showed me where they must have blocked you inside. I didn't want to disturb it and let them know you got out or get caught myself. I know this other way here, but knew I would have to dig a little to reach you, so I hurried back and got a pickaxe and shovel."

"So, this tunnel was already here?" Shriya asks.

"Yes. Someone had dug it out a long ago. One of my goats found it years ago. I went looking for her and she had eaten away the vegetation that had covered the entrance. The hole had been partly filled in, but I could see there was a cavern or something and I was curious about what it could be, so I dug it out and found this place."

"Where does it lead?" Shriya asks.

"Deep down inside the cliff."

"You've been down there?"

Enrique hesitates. "Yes, and what you are looking for is not there."

"How do you know?" Miguel asks.

"Oh, there is some treasure they are finding in the waters below, I'm sure, but they think the rest is covered by the collapse of the cliff," Enrique says. "Maybe there is some, but it will be a lot of work to try to get it and much of it is gone."

"Where did it go?" Shriya asks.

"Someone found it. Probably whoever built this tunnel and sealed the fort, I don't know. If you could still follow this tunnel down, it would bring you to a cavern at the level of the sea where the treasure must have been, but I believe most of it is gone now and the cavern roof has fallen in since then."

Juan Manuel leads Good Boy out of the tunnel into the light and heat of the sun, and onto a field of piled stones with a seaside cliff on one side and trees on the other. Good Boy wonders if he would have been better off staying underground.

"How did you find this place?" he asks Juan Manuel.

"The shepherd knew. I thought he would dig out the side where the people with Zonda blocked you in."

Good Boy frowns. "Zonda. Why do the good ones always have bad people?"

"I don't know. I didn't even know that was common. Hey, if you smiled a little more, and with me to introduce you, I'd bet you'd do pretty well with a goat."

"It might come to that." Good Boy says. "The shepherd probably came around here because he didn't want to risk being seen by the other men."

"Yeah, that makes sen...." Juan Manuel trails off as he smells the air. "You smell someone?"

"Yeah, there's another person behind the trees and I can smell that he's about to attack."

A creaking and cracking sound comes from the same direction as the smell.

"How can you tell he's about to attack?" Juan Manuel asks.

"He has the action smell."

"What is that?"

"A smell they give off when they're going to run or fight."

The people step out of the tunnel and Enrique shuts off the lantern. Good Boy barks a warning and they all look up as the sounds from the trees gets louder.

"Flank!" Good Boy says to Juan Manuel. "Your side!"

Juan Manuel hops up some of the stones as a tough-looking man emerges swiftly in their direction from under some growth. Good Boy barks and snarls and lunges at the man, who points a gun at him.

Before Miguel can raise the rifle to his shoulder, Juan Manuel charges down the rocks with three swift leaps and the man turns to look too late to react as he takes a goat skull to the side of his face, flinging him several meters into a large stone block. Good Boy barks with compliment and triumph.

"He barely saw me coming!" Juan Manuel exults.

"I call it the distract attack," Good Boy says, "but the people at my school called it a flanking attack."

"I thought it only worked on chimpanzees."

"And jaguars."

"For that one, you were on the ground," Juan Manuel says. "The jaguar was ready to kill you."

"Yes, but it was distracted!"

Juan Manuel looks at Shriya, who is taking the rifle off of the compressed person while Enrique ties him up and Miguel scans the area with his rifle for more people.

"I like this situation better," Juan Manuel says.

"So do I," Good Boy agrees.

Shriya stands and looks intensely into the trees, trying to see anything, but it's far too dark under the canopy of vegetation, so she gives up.

"They saved us again," she says, mostly to herself.

Enrique stops tying the man and unties the knots he already made.

"What are you doing?" Miguel asks.

"This man, he is already dead."

Juan Manuel looks at Good Boy. "Did I kill him?"

"Sounds like it." Good Boy sniffs the air. "And smells like it. His head must have smashed on that rock."

Juan Manuel looks at the body and sniffs. "What is that smell?"

"Blood."

"No, I know that one, the other smell."

"Brain. Really, it was the rock that killed him, not you," Good Boy says. "Are you upset?"

Juan Manuel looks up and around at everyone. Shriya pats his head and hugs him.

"No, I guess I'm getting used to it," he says.

Enrique finishes going through the man's pockets for any information and stands up. "We must go. Come, I have a place to hide." He looks at everyone one more time, "Where is the sloth?"

"She was with Charleston, the goat," Shriya says.

"She is probably safe in a tree," Enrique says. "Come now."

Shriya looks at Juan Manuel. "Where is Calypso?" she asks.

"Bahahahahaha."

"Go get her!" Shriya commands.

"Goats can be pretty smart, but do you think he understands such a thing?" Enrique asks.

"If I told you the things we've seen them do, you wouldn't believe me."

"Maybe I would," he says, looking where Juan Manuel had been waiting to charge the dead man.

"Do you know where Calypso is?" Good Boy asks Juan Manuel.

"She's in a tree around the other side."

"I need to stay with the people—they have guns, but they don't seem to have working noses," Good Boy says. "Are you going to be fine without me?"

"Me?" Juan Manuel asks, "it's the bad people who should worry!"

"Don't go easy on 'em!" Good Boy growls through a grin.

"No problem there."

Juan Manuel heads into the trees in the direction of the other side of the fort and everyone else follows Enrique through a path in the forest.

Juan Manuel finds the tree where he left Calypso and stands against it to wait for her. "We need to go!" he yells up to her.

"Where?" Calypso asks. "What about Good Boy and Shriya?"

"They're free. The shepherd dug them out from the other side. I killed a person."

"What?"

"It's been quite a day."

"You killed a person?"

"Well, Good Boy says it was the rock," Juan Manuel says, "but I knocked him into it."

"The shepherd?" Calypso asks.

"No, it was a bad person who attacked us."

"The one with Zonda?"

"No, someone we never saw before."

Calypso holds an extra-long blink. "There are too many people."

"Definitely too many bad ones," Juan Manuel agrees. "This one was hiding in the forest and the people didn't notice. When he started to charge them, Good Boy made like he was going to attack, but that was a distraction. I was waiting on the side where he didn't notice me and I leaped down on him."

"So, you killed him," Calypso says, reaching out to climb onto his back.

"Yes, but I only wanted to knock him down."

She locks her claws on Juan Manuel's collar and grips his fur with her back claws. "That's what you did."

"Yes, but I didn't intend for him to die."

"So, the rock killed him."

"The rock can't do anything," Juan Manuel says. "I knocked him into it."

"Eh, whichever. Where are we going?"

"To find everyone else."

"OK."

Juan Manuel goes back to the tunnel to pick up their trail.

Calypso smells blood and her eyes follow her nose to a blurry figure on the ground. "Is that the dead person?"

Flies buzz around them to see if they're edible, and Juan Manuel swats at them with his tail, so they return to the easier meal of the dead man. Juan Manuel aims his nose at the trees. "Yeah, that's the one. Let's go, I found the trail."

"Oof, yeah, I can smell them, too. People stink."

"Do you ever feel bad about that big monkey you knocked out of the tree?" Juan Manuel asks.

"You mean the chimpaneezee?"

"Yeah, chimpanzee, that's it!"

"No. Sloths fall all the time. If the giant monkeys can't take a fall, they should stay out of the trees," Calypso says. "And not mistreat my friends. Do you feel bad about them? Or those dogs you fought?"

"Did that dog die?" Juan Manuel asks.

"I don't know, but you stabbed him with your horn."

"No, I was defending my friends."

"You feel bad about this person, though?" Calypso asks.

"I don't know. The other ones were a fight in the open. This time I was being sneaky. Doesn't seem fair."

"Fair?" Calypso asks, sniffing the air. "Guns aren't fair. People aren't fair."

"No, I guess not. It still doesn't feel right." They walk on in silence until Juan Manuel realizes he's not going to get another comment from Calypso without further prompting. "Do you understand, though?"

"No," she says. "What about that jaguar?"

"That jaguar didn't die."

"You got it by surprise."

"Yeah, but I had to save Good Boy."

"I don't understand the difference." Calypso says.

"I don't either, but I feel different."

"Hm."

"I shouldn't expect you to understand if I don't." Juan Manuel says after a few more moments of silence have passed between them.

"Maybe it's how Good Boy feels he failed by not saving Pablo even though he's happy that it allowed him to save us,"

Calypso says. "Sometimes, we can feel multiple ways about one thing at the same time."

"The same way we are your friends," Juan Manuel says, "but you like to spend so much time alone in the trees."

"Yes, that's another good example."

The forest ends at a well-trod field smelling of goats. A small stucco house with a corrugated metal roof is on their left, with the goat smell coming from beyond it in the same direction. They head toward the house and Good Boy comes running over to them.

"Where is Shriya?" Calypso asks.

"The people are all in the house."

A few kids call to Juan Manuel from the goat pen and he calls back.

"I'm going to hang out with the goats for a little while," he tells them.

Good Boy steps alongside and Calypso climbs onto his back. "We'll get you if anything happens," she says, watching Juan Manuel hop over and do a little circular dance, which the kids imitate from behind the fence. Stepping back, then a quick leap, and he's over the fence with the rest of the goats. Calypso blinks and smiles, understanding what it means to be part of a herd, if only for a moment.

"Juan Manuel is great with the other goats," Good Boy says. "The kids really love him."

"He is lovable," Calypso agrees. "Should we see what the people are doing?"

Enrique and Shriya are seated around a small wood table in a room to the right side of the entry door, drinking tea. Miguel stands behind them looking at framed pictures on a bookshelf on the back wall. On the right is a kitchen, on the left is a bedroom. Good Boy's nose tells him that the bathroom is off of the kitchen. He walks over and sits next to Shriya's chair. Shriya reaches down to pet his head and Calypso pulls herself up to the back of the chair while Enrique leans back with a cup of tea to talk.

"The treasure is a curse," he says. "I hope nobody finds it, although it attracts the kind of people who cannot understand that such a thing can only lead to misery. It was taken by the Conquistadors at the behest of the Devil, its false promises of wealth and happiness are there to trap men's souls, a shining lure like an angler fish."

He looks at Shriya's unmoved, but polite face and chuckles, pointing his cup toward her. "I can see you humor me, but look at the men here searching for it now and how they are men of lost souls. Maybe you don't believe in the Devil and that is OK, I can tell that you are a smart person. Forget about the Devil and consider the history: the Spanish murdered for it, the pirates murdered for it, for centuries men have given up their lives searching for it, and now men are here who are willing to kill and die for it. They will not find the treasure, but they will find the curse and it will destroy them. I do not want this for any of you."

"We're not here for the treasure," Shriya says, "we're here for our friend who is being held by those men."

"Good Boy," Calypso waves to get his attention, "the shepherd is talking about the Devil things."

"I know."

"We might need Juan Manuel for this—he fought one of those things. What is he saying about them?"

"I don't know."

"If your friend is one of them," Enrique continues, eyeing Shriya over the rim of his cup, "then I am afraid that he's doomed."

Shriya puts down her tea. "He isn't one of them, he is being held because he thinks he knows where the treasure is and I think he must have found these men to help him get it and they turned on him. He's arrogant, not evil."

"Why didn't he notify the Archaeological National Commission?" Enrique asks. "If it is found, it is their property."

"Well, he . . . didn't want to lose it to the government."

"It sounds like he wanted it for himself."

"You don't understand," Shriya says, "he's a dreamer. Imagine finding a lost pirate treasure through the eyes of a child, not a thief."

Enrique shakes his head. "Whether he is a thief or a child-like dreamer, he is stuck with the same consequences of his decisions. Do not get dragged down with him. Now, these men will soon find you gone and their comrade dead. I am pleading with you to leave this place. Take my ATV back to your car, leave it at the end of the trail, and go far away."

"What about you?" Miguel asks, pulling out another chair and sitting down.

"The Devil has already made his claim for me and I await whatever may come."

"That doesn't make any sense, if you're afraid of these men, come with us," Miguel says. "Even if it's just for a few days until we can get the authorities involved and you can come back."

Shriya shakes her head. "We're not leaving Rondo here to be killed. If the authorities show up, he's dead for sure."

"I don't want to die for Rondo, do you?" Miguel says. "You saw what kind of men we're dealing with."

"And I saw a goat kill one of them," Shriya says quietly.

"I know these animals are incredible, but a goat taking one isolated man by surprise is luck as much as pluck," Miguel says. "I don't think we should push our luck any further."

"I might not believe in the Devil," Shriya says fiercely, "but I believe in us and that we can get him back."

"It's not important if the Devil is real or speaks for the evil within people," Enrique interjects. "You are good people with amazing animals friends, but these men are killers and killers prey on the good."

Shriya leans back and almost squashes one of Calypso's arms against the seat. She turns and pets her as an apology that Calypso accepts with a slow blink.

"You know they won't find it," Shriya says, turning back to Enrique.

114

"They might, but they won't find it there."

"And you know that because you already found it."

"What we found was a curse," Enrique says, "and my wife has already been stricken down by it. I'm still here because I agreed to keep anyone else from ever finding it."

"Agreed with who?" Miguel asks.

Enrique looks at him and says nothing.

Good Boy's ears rotate toward the sound of the hollow thunk and scuff of a human kicking and stumbling on a root outside. He leaps to attention, barking an alert, and Calypso climbs down to his back. A goat bleats a warning from the field and a big dog barks outside. More goats bleat in desperation.

Immediately on his feet, face pale, Enrique looks at his guests.

"You must go now," he says. "I should not have spoken aloud of the curse. Come! May God be with you."

Shriya picks up Calypso and Enrique leads them all to the corner of the dining room where a bookcase that's more photos and mementos than books faces them. A framed picture of Enrique and his late wife hang on the opposite wall. He pulls down on the top of the picture frame, there's a click, and the bookcase pops away from the wall on one side. He pulls that side out a bit to clear the wall, then pushes on the opposite side, pivoting it open to reveal a dark tunnel.

"You have lights on your phones?"

"Yes," Shriya says.

"Good, I don't want to turn on the main lights and give away the secret. When you get to the bottom, go to the right—it will take you to a shed on the far side of the goat pen. The ATV is in there. Wait until it is safe and go!"

"What about you?" Shriya asks.

"Don't think about me, just get free and call for the authorities. Make sure someone takes care of my goats if the Devil may take me. Go!" He pushes them into the tunnel and rotates the bookcase closed.

Miguel turns on his phone light to illuminate the stairway and Shriya lowers Calypso onto Good Boy's back to have her hands free.

"What is happening?" Calypso asks.

"The bad men are outside and I think this is a hiding place."

"What about the shepherd?"

"I think he's staying behind to meet the bad men."

"That doesn't sound safe."

"No."

"What about Juan Manuel?" Calypso says. "Do you think the people will hurt him?"

"No, but we're not going to leave him behind."

"Of course not. I heard another dog outside back there. I don't know for sure, but it might have been—"

"Yes," Good Boy says.

The stairs end at a perpendicular tunnel supported by wood columns and beams that remind Shriya of an old mine. She shines her phone light in either direction. The walls are covered in plaster. On the wall between every other column are unlit cast iron sconces.

The left side of the tunnel ends about four meters away at a plaster wall framed on the top and sides by wood supports. On their right is an open area with stacks of assorted items covered in dust.

"Do you think there are dead people in this one?" Calypso asks Good Boy. "I don't see any stone devils." She reaches out and catches a claw on one of the vertical wood supports. "This place is made from trees."

"I don't smell any dead people."

Shriya and Miguel stop to look at the stacks of stored items, which turn out to be old house stuff and tools.

Miguel quietly opens a few boxes to confirm the contents, and shrugs.

Shriya looks disappointed. "I thought we'd find the treasure in here," she whispers.

"Me, too," Miguel whispers back. "I think you are right, though, that Enrique found it. He said he's making sure nobody finds it again, so maybe he buried it somewhere else."

Calypso is completely uninterested in what the people are talking about. "We should get Juan Manuel," she says to Good Boy.

Good boy grunts and nudges Shriya down the tunnel toward some old stairs at the far end, about twenty meters down.

Reaching the end, Miguel takes his rifle out and carefully ascends the stairs. Pressing his ear to the wood trap door at the top, he can hear loud voices arguing and threatening, though he can't make out the words. He comes back down and whispers, "There's arguing. I think they have Enrique and—"

A door opens above them and several sets of heavy footsteps pound on the floor.

"Where are they, shepherd?" a voice snarls.

"I told you I do not know."

"Then why do you have their goat with the broken horn in the pen?"

"They sold him to me."

"Now you admit you saw them!"

"I never said I didn't see them," they hear Enrique say. "You said they killed one of your men and asked if I knew where they are and I told you I don't."

Shriya motions to Miguel like she's holding a rifle and aiming it at the men upstairs.

Miguel shakes his head and holds up three fingers to indicate that there are too many of them. The floor creaks as the men walk around the shed. There's a pop, followed by the sound of rushing air, then another, and another.

"What are you doing?" One of the men admonishes. "We might be able to use that!"

"So could the two we're looking for!"

A smack and a series of heavy thumps. They hear Enrique groan as he falls to the floor and Good Boy suppresses the urge to bark. Dirt falls through the cracks into the generous cobwebs

117

between the joists supporting the shed floor. Shriya silently mouths curses.

Good Boy glances up and back at Calypso, who looks at him with confusion. A grunt from above as Enrique is helped to his feet and a door slams as the men all leave the shed.

Miguel waits a minute before trying the trap door, propping it up a crack to see the shed is clear. Lifting the door until it is stopped by a length of cord just long enough to allow it to hold open, he waves for everyone to follow. Shriya takes Calypso so Good Boy can better climb the steep steps and emerges from the opening to see Miguel pointing to the flat tires of the ATV with a shaking head. She frowns and spots a hatchet on the wall, which she takes in case it's needed, cursing herself for having left the rifle that she had taken off the pirate at the cave back in Enrique's house.

Bang!

A gunshot a short distance away and everyone freezes for a moment. Goats bleat in fear and protest.

Shriya motions for Miguel to go back into the tunnel, letting him go first so she can pass Good Boy and Calypso down before closing the door behind them, and descending the stairs.

"I would bet that gunshot was Enrique," Miguel says, letting Calypso go on top of Good Boy.

"I won't bet against that."

"What do you think we should do?"

"I think we need to wait for nightfall," Shriya says.

"That's not a bad idea, but what if they stay here? It didn't look like there is much room on that sailboat for them all to sleep."

"Yeah," Shriya agrees, "maybe we wait until it's really late before sneaking back inside the house and, if we see them, we kill them in their sleep."

"Are you serious?"

She frowns. "No, I just realized that we would have to worry about their dog waking them up. Let's see if there's another gun or something else we can use."

118

"What happened to the other rifle from that guy Charleston killed?"

"I left it in the house," she says, shaking her head in disappointment.

Good Boy takes Calypso back down the tunnel. At the bottom of the house stairs, he smells something he doesn't recognize coming from the wall that closes off the other end of the tunnel. Following his nose to the dead end, it seems to be coming from around the bottom and he sniffs a narrow gap allowing air to escape.

"What is that?" Calypso asks.

"You smell it, too?"

"Yes, it smells a bit like big water, but there's something else, isn't there?"

"I don't know what that is," Good Boy says.

Shriya comes up quietly behind them, curious as to what they've noticed. Good Boy looks to her and Calypso blinks up at her before reaching out to claw the wall. Now Miguel stands behind them, looking nervously back to the stairway before giving Shriya a questioning look.

Shriya points at the floor where Good Boy is sniffing around before getting down to join him. She doesn't notice anything unusual and is about to dismiss it when she sees a spider run under the wall and disappear. Standing, she mouths and pantomimes that the wall might actually be a door to Miguel, who nods and looks for a possible trigger to open it.

Shriya pushes on it in several spots, but it feels completely solid, and knocking carefully upon it doesn't tell her whether or not there's a cavity behind it. Turning her head, she notices the sconce at the same time as Miguel, and they put their hands on it simultaneously.

She removes her hand and nods for Miguel to pull on it. It stays anchored firmly into the plaster. He motions to her with an asking expression if she thinks he should yank hard on it and she shrugs. He puts his hand back on it and is about to pull it hard

119

when she stops him with her hand on his and points to the next sconce down the wall just past the stairway.

She turns her palms up in doubt, so he decides to investigate that one, but it doesn't move without risking tearing it from the wall. Shriya frowns and reaches up for the first sconce again, feeling how substantially built it is for something that only needs to hold a lightbulb away from a wall. Under the circular wall mount, the wall has been scored away a little, with deeper scoring on the side closer to the dead end.

She checks Miguel's sconce to make sure it doesn't have the same markings. As she expects, there are no score marks behind it. Returning to the first sconce, she pulls the top toward the dead end to turn the sconce counterclockwise and it moves a little before seeming to bind up. Rotating it back and forth the few degrees of movement that it allows, she can feel that it is working on a pivot of some strength that is encountering mechanical resistance to turning any farther.

She motions for Miguel to come over to help turn it and, this time, it turns until they hear a heavy, dull click as if a spring-loaded latch has been released and the sconce stops. She aims the light around the dead end stone wall to see if it has moved. A crack has opened up between the dead end wall and the adjacent wood column on the sconce wall. She releases the sconce and it rotates itself back into its original position.

"Ooh, look at that," Calypso says.

Good Boy sticks his nose to the crack, trying to push his way through, but it's too heavy. Shriya presses her hand to it, which isn't enough, and she has to resort to leaning in with her shoulder. Slowly, the wall rotates inwards before she stops to shine her light around the opening to determine that it's safe.

Not seeing anything that might trigger a trap, Miguel helps her walk the door open wide enough for them to get inside. It's a fair sized room, about as large as the living quarters upstairs, and the walls are barely visible for the stacks of crates and large sedimentary stones with edges that glitter like minerals.

120

Shriya ushers everyone else in, looking back to make sure they haven't been discovered, then following them inside. The massive door looks to have once belonged to a bank before being installed in the tunnel and disguised with plaster. She wonders how Enrique had gotten it down there as she swings it shut behind them.

Turning the phone light to the room, Miguel flicks on a wall switch. He stares at the shining minerals they can now see are actually accretions of ocean sediment, precious stones, and gold.

"Oh. My. God." Miguel quietly breathes the words out.

Shriya nods and swallows, eyes wide to take in the vast expanse of treasure. "I had no idea there would be so much."

"This is what was left after the Spanish and the pirates recovered much of it?"

"And whatever might still be buried out there," Shriya says quietly, mouth open in shock.

The first small crate they look at is filled with a pile of gold coins topped by gemstones—mostly emeralds—that have either been freed of the sediment that still clings to the stacks in the rest of the vault, or had never accumulated sand.

Shriya weighs a chunk of stuck together gold coins in her hand. "Whoa, this is heavy!" she exclaims. "Most of it seems to be gold. And, of course, there are the crates."

"How big were these treasure galleons?" Miguel asks. "There must be millions or even billions here and I'm talking US dollars!" He shakes his head and whistles. "What do we do?"

Shriya puts the block back and shrugs. "I don't know. Maybe we could negotiate with them for Rondo. Or we could take some of it with us if we can escape tonight and turn it over to the government before pointing them in the direction of the bad guys." She wipes her hands on her thighs and considers for a moment.

"Either way, we're going to need the authorities since I can't see them negotiating with us in good faith. Once they know where it really is, what's to stop them from killing all of us? I think what we should do is set this crate of clean stones somewhere outside the vault and direct the pirates here to find it as proof that we know where it is and we don't tell them about the vault until they let Rondo go. Maybe we bury a few of the larger jewels somewhere for ourselves to get later."

Miguel holds up a stone with emeralds set into gold peeking out and puts it down again. "What about the curse?"

"The curse is human greed, and that exists whether there's Spanish gold around or not," Shriya says.

"What would you do with it?" Miguel asks.

"Send some to my parents, to the sloth rescue, maybe fund a few research grants. Oh, and I'd get myself a small sailboat." She gestures vaguely toward the fort. "I could also use a new car."

He nods. "Something fancy? Maybe some nice clothes?"

"I don't care about that—isn't it obvious?" She twirls in her old pants and tee shirt. "I would get something a little fancier than an old Corolla, though. Nothing extravagant, but I wouldn't mind something a little more comfortable, a little nicer. How about you?"

Miguel shakes his head. "I don't want any of it."

"You're not even going to dream about what you could do with it?"

"That's not a dream, that's a nightmare. How many lives has this treasure claimed?" Miguel nods in the direction of where Enrique was shot.

"Maybe you're right," Shriya agrees after a moment. "No, you *are* right. And it's not like either of us will be starving without it." She takes a long look at a case of freed jewels and sighs.

Miguel nods. "This kind of thing is fun for movies, but this is real life. Even if we could make off with this, how would we exchange it for money without attracting all kinds of bad attention?"

Shriya frowns. "That happened before we even found it."

"Isn't this just stone?" Calypso asks Good Boy.

"Seems like it. I think it comes from the bottom of the big water."

"Yeah, it smells like that, but why are the people going on about it?"

"I don't know."

Calypso casts her nose around and feels the energy of the room. "I don't like it in here. We need to get out and get Juan Manuel."

"The bad people might still be out there," Good Boy says.

Shriya walks to the door and realizes that the handle she thought might unlatch it is locked. "Uh, we might have a problem," she says quietly.

"What is it?" Miguel asks, putting down a chunk of encrusted treasure with a gold sculpture partially sticking out, and going over to her.

"The door is locked. How do we unlatch the door to get out of here?"

"Maybe there's another hidden lever?"

She taps the large combination dial on the door, the only thing there is.

Miguel's eyes panic. He looks around the room for something that might give the combination, but nothing stands out.

"This must be what Enrique meant about preventing anyone else from having it," Shriya says.

"There must be something in here . . . what if he came in and forgot the number himself?" Miguel looks at Good Boy, who sits down and whimpers with concern. Calypso puts her arms around his neck.

Shriya stares at the door in thought, noticing that there's a column of circular arrows drawn onto the door in marker reminding which way the dial would have to be set to unlock it. From the top: rotating to the right, to the left with a double arrow, and to the right again.

"What if he didn't have to worry about forgetting?" she asks Miguel.

"Yeah, why would he lock himself in here?" Miguel agrees. "That seems stupid. We should have stuck something in the doorway to prevent it from latching."

"No, I mean, because the combination would be something he would never forget, unlike the rotation of the dial that he wrote down here. If you were worried about forgetting something simple, like which way the dial turns so you don't get trapped in here, the combination would have to be something he wouldn't possibly forget to not also write it down."

"You mean, like his wife's birthday?"

"Exactly. Dammit, that doesn't do us any good!"

Miguel puts his hand gently on Shriya's arm to guide her away from the door and proceeds to spin the dial according to the marker directions. He pulls the release lever. It won't move, so he tries again. Nothing.

"Damn."

"What are you trying to do?" Shriya asks.

"That was his wife's birthday."

"How do you know that?"

"From the photo upstairs." Miguel spins the dial to reset it and make another attempt.

"You remembered that?"

"She had almost the same birthday as my mother. Different year, of course." He tries to pull the lever, but it still doesn't open.

"Are you sure you have the right year?" Shriya asks. "Maybe that's not it."

"I might have the wrong year. I can't remember if it's 2019 or 18. Let me try the 18." Miguel resets and spins the dial again.

"Wait, how could it be either?"

His tentative hand reaches for the lever again, Shriya holds her breath. A stiff sliding sound and the door clunks. Shriya yanks the door away from the jam just enough to prevent it from possibly relocking. The pain of pulling too hard makes her immediately regret it.

124

Good Boy barks in applause and stands, wagging his tail. Miguel breaks off a piece of wood from one of the cases and sticks it between the door and the jamb to hold it while Shriya puts her ear to the crack to listen for anyone outside. Dead quiet. She immediately frowns at herself for thinking of that particular term. "I don't hear anyone," she whispers.

"Good. Your arm OK?" Miguel whispers back, seeing her rubbing the top of her arm.

"I should have pulled slowly."

"Kind of sad."

"It's fine, just getting old."

"No," Miguel says, "I mean the combination wasn't his wife's birthday, it was the day she died."

"How did you know that?"

"It was on the frame with her birthday. I did the math to figure out how old she had been, so that stuck it in my mind, though I forgot the exact year because she was forty three by the year, but really only forty two years old because of the month. Then I confused myself wondering whether she was actually forty three and should have been forty four."

"From what he told us," Shriya says, "he must have built this before she died and changed the combo after. I guess he really did blame it on a curse."

"I think he was right," Miguel says quietly.

Shriya puts her finger to her lips and ducks down, carefully pulling the door open, and peeking outside. Good Boy sticks his nose to check for bad people. He snorts that it's clear, but the people feel they need to check for themselves. He looks up at Calypso to share his disappointment, but she doesn't seem to notice. Miguel kicks the door stop out of the way and picks up the case of freed gold and gemstones, then they all quietly escape the hidden vault, the door locking behind them automatically when they close it.

Bowlegged from the weight and cradling the flimsy crate in his arms, Miguel walks it over to the covered boxes and slides it under the canvas next to them.

Ear to the hidden bookcase door of Enrique's house, Shriya can't detect any sign of life behind it. Miguel aims his rifle at chest height and Shriya nods before taking a breath to lift the catch for the door and ease it open, an awkward move with the bookcase swinging out at one side, then rotating open over the stairs.

The house is abandoned. Everything is strewn about on the floor, presumably by the thieves. There is no sound except for the distressed bleating of goats outside. Good Boy barks and Shriya puts a calming hand on his head to tell him to keep quiet, but the shaking in her hand leaves him feeling more anxious instead.

Calypso notices the mess. "Did a big wind come through here?" she asks Good Boy.

"I think it was the bad people."

"It's like a tree got shook and everyone fell out. Are the bad people gone? The shepherd isn't going to like this."

"I don't know where the bad people are," Good Boy says. "Enrique the shepherd is dead."

Calypso looks around the room. "The bad people killed him?"

"Yes."

"Where?"

"Outside."

"Oh, now I hear—the goats are afraid."

"And angry," Good Boy adds.

"Do you hear Juan Manuel?"

"Yes, he's yelling about the bad people, but I think they're gone."

"That's good," Calypso says. "If he's yelling, he's still alive."

Shriya checks down the road through the dusty old front window blinds. There are no people in sight. "I think they're gone," she tells Miguel.

He nods in agreement from his window facing the goat pen. "The goats are very agitated."

"Yeah, I can hear that," Shriya says, "and I don't like what it might mean."

"Me, neither."

Shriya turns to the wall behind the table where they had been drinking tea just a short time ago. "Dammit," she curses, practically spitting the word.

"What?"

"They took the other rifle."

They go outside and Good Boy runs for the goat pen. Juan Manuel immediately squeezes through the herd to him.

"They shot him," Juan Manuel bleats, "they just shot him and dumped him, they shot him for no reason!"

"Bad people don't need a reason," Good Boy says.

"Yeah, well they gave *me* one!"

Calypso looks over the scared and angry faces of the goats and it breaks her heart. "We need to get away from this horrible place and take the goats with us," she says. "Miguel has all those other goats they could live with."

"They had a perfectly good place here!" Juan Manuel says, stomping in rage.

"Not anymore." Calypso looks over the herd. "Why are the people like this?"

"I don't know and I don't care anymore!" Juan Manuel bleats angrily. "I want to push them all over that cliff!"

Good Boy narrows his eyes and his fur stands on end. "We just might do that."

Juan Manuel calms slightly. "What are you thinking?"

"I don't know yet. I need to get a better look at what we're dealing with."

Enrique's body is face down near the goat pen. Shriya runs over to check for a pulse before noticing the bloody mess of his hair and skull. There's nothing that can be done.

127

"What do we do?" Miguel asks, surveying the area. "I don't want to leave him like this, especially in front of the goats, but if we bury him and they come back, they'll know we were here."

Shriya looks at the fear and anger in the eyes of the goats. "We don't have time to bury him. Maybe we could at least cover him up with something? The bastards already know we're around."

Miguel wipes his hands on his pants. "I'll grab a sheet from inside."

```
          /\    /\                                      ~ \    / ~
 ----- \ 0    0 / --------- |||--/o) _ (o\--||| --------- (        ) -----
          \    /                                           \ /
           \  /                                             \/
            \/
```

"Are we leaving now?" Calypso asks Juan Manuel, watching Good Boy walking to the cliff and looking down.

"Depends on what Good Boy sees," he says.

"I think it depends on what Shriya does."

"I don't know what she is going to do, but Good Boy and I aren't leaving until we know if there's something we can do to the bad people."

"The bad people have all of those guns and Zonda. What can we do?"

"Whatever Good Boy comes up with," Juan Manuel says. "If he comes up with anything."

"It's the boat," Good Boy says as Juan Manuel steps up next to him and looks down at the beach below. Someone on the barge screams and is held down by other men. One of them laughs at the distraught man as the Speedwell is pulled up alongside. Some other people are paddling an open boat the short distance to the beach.

Shriya and Miguel crouch down beside Good Boy, Juan Manuel, and Calypso, using a mound over a remnant of the old fort wall as cover. Shriya watches the Speedwell while Miguel uses the binoculars, careful to shield them. The small boat is pulled onto the beach and several heavy-looking crates are handed off from the Speedwell to a man on the barge. One of the men on the barge hops inside before the Speedwell backs into the surf and turns to speed out of the cove.

Miguel hands the binoculars to Shriya and points at the barge. She scans over the diving gear on the barge to focus on a person sitting on the floor in the far corner looking frightened.

"I think that's Rondo," she whispers to Miguel, handing back the binoculars and leaning away from the cliff until she feels she's safe enough from being seen from below to stand. Miguel does the same and scans the area for bad guys again, but doesn't see any.

Miguel checks his phone. "There's no phone signal out here," he says without surprise, "We should run down to the car."

Shriya checks her own phone. "Mine's got nothing, either. Let's go." She turns to the animals and slaps her leg. Good Boy runs over and Juan Manuel follows with Calypso on his back. Feeling the human's fear, Good Boy stays a short distance ahead of the group in case of a problem.

Zonda! At the end of the trail, Good Boy detects her scent, along with that of the car, and barks as she comes running out of the forest unleashed. They jump at each other excitedly and she runs into the forest, Good Boy following her. Calypso blinks slowly and nods from her perch on Juan Manuel's back. "That's nice to see," she says.

"Yeah," Juan Manuel agrees. "Now I don't have to try to find him a female goat,"

"Why are the people unhappy about it?" Calypso looks to Miguel, who is slinging the rifle from off his shoulder and to Shriya, who is taking a hatchet out of a loop on her pack.

"Buca!" Shriya yells as Rico stands up from behind their car and points a rifle at her.

"Drop it, pandejo!" Rico yells at Miguel.

Miguel reluctantly lays the rifle on the ground and Shriya drops the hatchet. Its blade sticking into the ground.

"Oh, that's what they were afraid of," Calypso says. "We need Good Boy!"

"He's distracted by love!" Juan Manuel complains. "Hang on!"

Calypso locks her claws around his collar, and they bolt out of sight into the forest in a few swift leaps.

Rico ignores the animals. "Back up," he tells Shriya and Miguel. They step back and he comes forward, taking up the rifle and tucking the hatchet into the back of his waistband. "How did you get out of the fort?" he asks.

"We broke out," Miguel says. "You're not much of an architect."

"Or even a beaver," Shriya says.

Rico grunts a laugh and cocks his head toward Shriya's car. "Get in." They walk in front of him to the back doors.

"In the *front* seats," he says and looks at Shriya. "You drive."

Shriya gets in and starts the car. "Where are we going?" she asks.

"Back to the fort."

Rico opens the passenger rear door and sits inside. He whistles and Zonda comes running out of the forest to leap into the backseat. "You want to see Rondo? Let's go."

"I don't know if this car can make it up the trail," Shriya says.

"Such negative thinking! The car just needs some willpower, like that little train in the children's story. *I think I can, I think I can.*" Rico laughs before cutting himself off. "Make it work." He says threateningly.

Good Boy busts out of the forest only to see the car drive up the trail.

"Baaaaaaah!" Juan Manuel calls from behind him.

Good Boy stops running after the car then starts again, then stops, and runs back to Calypso and Juan Manuel.

"I failed again!" he whimpers, tail between his legs.

"How did you fail?" Juan Manuel asks him.

"Because I was playing chase with Zonda!"

"He had a gun! Why do you think I ran?"

"How could you fight him with her on your back?" Good Boy says, unconsoled. Calypso turns away and Good Boy immediately wishes he could take back what he said.

"Sorry," he tells her, "I only meant that he couldn't maneuver with you on him." She doesn't respond and he tries to lick her face, but she turns her head the other way before pushing his nose off of her, then she relents and scratches his head in forgiveness.

"The people are going to kill Shriya like they killed Pablo!" Good Boy says.

"They are the same people?" Juan Manuel asks.

"Yes!"

"That isn't good."

"I was trying to get Zonda away from him."

"You were certainly trying to do *something* with Zonda." Juan Manuel says.

"Yeah, that was going to be how," Good Boy grumbles.

"So what do we do?" Calypso asks.

"There are too many people there and they have guns," Good Boy says. "If Zonda was with us, we could come up with something, but without her on our side, we don't stand a chance."

"Then, we need more people," Calypso says. "Good people."

"Finding those will be the hardest thing yet," Juan Manuel says with a stomp.

Calypso looks back down the road to town. "We go back the way we got here in the car."

"That's very far away," Good Boy says. "And the car moves faster than we do."

Juan Manuel nods. "We better start moving."

They're not too far down the road when they hear a loud, large engine coming their way. Good Boy steps into the cover of the tree line and Juan Manuel follows his lead as a box truck on squeaking suspension bounces and clatters to a stop about ten dog-lengths in front of them. A mean looking person in the front cab looks down a dirt side road cutting through the forest and indicates to the driver. The truck turns and disappears behind the trees.

"Did you see that person?!" Good Boy asks Calypso.

She looks at the blur of vegetation. "No."

"I did," Juan Manuel says. "It was one of the men from the town where they were going to eat me."

"Exactly."

"What do you think they're doing down there?"

"I think we should find out," Good Boy says.

"How do you know it's the same person?" Calypso asks. "I think we should keep heading down this road to get help."

"It's definitely the same person," Good Boy says, "and we're too far from where the other people are. The bad men are down there."

"Is this about the men who killed Pablo," Calypso asks him, "or helping Shriya?"

"It can be both," Good Boy says. "Maybe this leads back to the beach at the bottom of the cliff where the bad men are probably taking Shriya."

"And Miguel," Juan Manuel reminds them.

"Yes, but I thought we didn't want to go there because there are too many people with guns!" Calypso says.

"Yeah," Good Boy says, "but they won't expect us from this direction."

Calypso taps Juan Manuel for help, but he snorts in agreement with Good Boy. "I don't know how we were going to get other people back in the town to help us, anyway."

Calypso blinks slowly in resignation. "Fine."

In the Air Tonight

The road is wider than the path to the fort, yet the width of the box truck means it still has to push its way through the partially overgrown vegetation crowding in from the sides. Though the friends follow far enough back to stay out of sight, the truck is easy to follow by the noise alone as it squeaks its way slowly toward the unknown.

The smell of the sea gets stronger well before the sound of the waves finally reveal the truck's final destination at the water's edge. The ticking and rumbling of the truck's engine goes silent and Good Boy leads Juan Manuel into the forest alongside the road so that they can see what the people are up to from a concealed position in the dark of the forest. The tree line ends several dog lengths away from where the truck is parked on the edge of a sandy beach.

Two men have rolled up the back of the truck and are unpacking small crates from the back to carry them to a makeshift dock. Tied up to the dock is the Speedwell, and a third man takes the dropped off crates from the dock and puts them on board the boat.

"That's the boat!" Good Boy says. "We can use it to rescue Shriya."

Calypso squints, but can just make out what appears to be a boat floating at a dock, nothing more. "Are you sure it's the same boat?"

"That's the one."

"Which way would we go to get her?" Calypso asks.

"What? Back the way we came."

"We came from the road. The road turned around. I don't know which way *back* would be."

Good Boy looks both ways and points to his left. "That way."

"Are you sure?"

"Yeah, can't you feel it?"

Calypso tries to feel the direction for a moment, but her sense of direction isn't good for such large expanses. "No."

"Well, we didn't walk back around past where they have Shriya and the big water is in front of us, so it has to be that way."

"OK."

"None of this even matters unless we figure out how to get the boat away from the people." Juan Manuel says. "It's too far to take them by surprise with a charge."

"You're going to walk right up to them." Good Boy turns toward Calypso, "Both of you."

She blinks slowly at him, then looks at the blurry people moving to and from the dock.

"Then what?" Juan Manuel asks.

"You distract them and I'll come out from behind the truck and attack them from behind, then you get her to the boat and I'll join you."

"*If* you can join us," Juan Manuel says, "There are four of them, including the guy on the dock!"

"Yeah, I can count, too. They're carrying boxes that look heavy. They won't be ready for an attack."

"What about the one in the boat?"

"He'll come out to help the others," Good Boy says.

"You hope!"

"Yes. When he comes out, Calypso, you have to drop off," Good Boy says, setting their plan. "Juan Manuel, see if you can smash him first. If it doesn't go our way, we go back into the forest. I don't think they'll follow us far as it looks like they're doing something they think is more important."

"This sounds terrible," Juan Manuel says.

"Yes," Good Boy agrees, "But do you have another idea?"

"I say we go back to where the people are," Calypso says. "If this doesn't work."

"If it doesn't work," Calypso says, "*and* we can escape."

"OK, so we're doing this," Juan Manuel mutters. "How do I approach? Every person we meet is surprised to see her riding us. With her on my back, the man from the town is going to recognize us."

"Yeah . . . I don't know if that's good or bad," Good Boy says. "If they recognize you, they might all gather around and pay more attention. If they don't recognize you, they might ignore you so you can get right up to the boat."

"They will recognize me with her."

"I'll ride Good Boy," Calypso says.

"He needs to be free to attack."

Good Boy watches the people for a few moments. "They're not paying attention to our side of the truck," he says. "Calypso, what if I bring you to the truck and come back for you?"

"What if we have to retreat?" Juan Manuel asks.

"I'll cover the retreat while you get her and escape."

"What does that mean?" Juan Manuel asks. "If you could cover a retreat, we wouldn't need to do it!"

"Don't worry about what happens to me."

Calypso stares at the truck and the blurry people. "We don't retreat, we get the boat. Bring me to the truck."

Juan Manuel takes a deep breath and snorts it out before trotting to the unloading area. Walking up to the back of the truck, he stands on his hind legs to look inside. It smells odd. One of the men returning to the truck for another case yells at him and waves to scare him off, but Juan Manuel bleats a curse in response before hopping inside.

"Hey, get out of here!" the man inside the truck yells, gesturing as if to push Juan Manuel away. The two men carrying the crates put them down and run to the truck to help, Good Boy takes the opportunity to bring Calypso to the truck.

She climbs onto the front tire and reaches up to get hold of the door handle. The smell from the nearby fuel tank irritates her nose. Juan Manuel protests loudly from inside, leaping onto a stack of crates to dodge the men as they try to grab his legs.

"No! No! No!" The men all yell. The two men outside of the truck climb in to help the third corner Juan Manuel.

Good Boy stands hidden in front of the truck, waiting for the man on the boat to look away. Suddenly the man yells out, "Hey, what's going on, you morons? It's dark and we have several loads to make!" With only shouting men and a goat as a response, the man swears at his coworkers, steps onto the temporary dock, and runs for the truck.

Seeing the man leave the boat, Good Boy stands in shock for a moment before gaining his senses and going back for Calypso.

"Are we retreating?"

"No, Juan Manuel has them all distracted, let's go!"

She grabs his collar and climbs onto his back, and he races to the boat. Letting Calypso off to ready the boat, Good Boy bites the top loop of the bow line that holds the boat to the dock and pulls, feeling the end slip out from the knot, he pulls it loose. Calypso is releasing the midship line as he passes her to take care of the stern line.

A loud crash comes from the truck as Good Boy releases the line and runs to help Juan Manuel. One of the men rolls out the back and lands on his shoulders on the ground with Juan Manuel leaping over him and around the far side of the truck. Another man jumps down to check on the fallen man and a mix of laughing and cursing comes from inside the truck as Juan Manuel rounds the front and makes straight for the boat.

"Wake it up!" Good Boy yells, executing a fast turn and heading back to the boat.

Calypso thinks for a moment, hits the stick for the battery switch, and then pushes the control stick forward to lower the motor. Juan Manuel hops onto the seat and into the back to make room for Good Boy as he leaps inside.

Some music starts up with synth drums. A slow, quiet beat that is soon overlaid by an ominous sound that coalesces into a melody that follows the beat. The boat floats away from the dock and Calypso hits the start button to awaken the motor. The men jump out of the truck and run for the dock shouting rage while, in the boat, the voice of a man over the speakers starts to sing a quiet threat of his own. Calypso shoves the throttle forward. The boat clunks into gear and powers toward fate.

The moon and stars shine off the tips of the waves and the wake that leaps away from the cutting bow as it retreats from its sides. The port bow light casts a red glow on the left of the nose, a steady beacon within the dancing reflections of the night sky on the glossy deck and hull. The wind blows gently through the friends' fur.

Juan Manuel stands behind the seat with his head over the back, staring through the windshield with uncharacteristic stoicism. Good Boy turns to Calypso, intently looking ahead, lost in concentration, heavy with purpose. The outboard motor, hidden between the tail fins, kicks up a rooster tail—white glitter in the dreamtime's reflections. Good Boy shares a nod with Juan Manuel, then looks back through the windshield.

"How far have we got?" Calypso asks without moving her straining eyes from straight ahead, the sound of the question in her friends' heads like a disembodied voice carried on the wind that flicks around the windshield.

"Not far. I'll tell you when to turn toward the beach," Good Boy says mechanically, his mind lost in thought of his training, of how he was supposed to do anything to protect Pablo, to shrug off bullets and keep attacking until he could no longer move. If he was to lose three legs, he should have dragged himself at the enemy with the last one. Then there was the day when the bad men came for Pablo and he got out of there without taking a single bullet, merely barking at them, no different than a decorative dog playing pretend predator.

Good Boy looks at Calypso and thinks about how she could have stayed in the trees but instead here she is, in danger today because of *him*—his failure to protect Shriya. Juan Manuel would have been better off with other goats, but he's along with them because of *him*. They aren't trained, they aren't predators, and they're about to take on the most dangerous animals in existence. They're here to help Shriya or die trying, and they trust they have a chance of succeeding because they think they're following a fearless trained attack dog into battle.

Fearless, no, his inner voice agrees, but who led the charges against Thundersloth that resulted in a revolt? Who threw himself on the fearsome chimpanzees?

They all did, he snorts at himself.

No, they know the risk, and they're following him. It's not about the past, it's about the future. He is the dog that fought the chimpanzees and he is the dog that will fight the people.

They could really use Thundersloth.

Calm and solemn with the creaking wood crates under his kneeling legs, Juan Manuel's life memories scroll through his mind's eye, fully prepared for that stream to be coming to an end soon. From his days as a kid jumping carefree and causing mischief to the day of the flood when the rest of his herd was washed away and killed, only for him to be rescued from a bent tree he had been able to climb by people who intended to eat him.

That same night, a mean-looking dog and a strange little sloth showed up behind the building where he had been tied up to await his fate. The day he lost his herd, he found his best friends. Juan Manuel wonders at the unpredictable twists of life. The things he's seen and done with his friends since that day are things no goat could have ever imagined. He wonders if any of it was even real. Maybe he had died with his herd and this whole thing has been some kind of strange death dream.

"Good Boy?" Juan Manuel says quietly into the moonlight on the water.

Good Boy takes a slow breath in before answering. "Yeah?"

"I need to know something . . . that this isn't a death dream, that I didn't die and imagine all this. Everything that we've been through, it was real, wasn't it?"

"Yeah, it was," Good Boy nods. "Every incredible moment. What's wrong, goat?"

"Nothing, dog."

Calypso pushes the throttle to its stop, the drum in the music kicks up, the long nose of the boat comes off the tops of the waves, pounding heavily upon the top of the next one, then up its crest and splashing down again. The boat feels uncharacteristically heavy, especially in the front, and the engine sounds strained even though the boat is moving slower than she expects—it fells tired, like her.

The boat is approaching a rocky outcrop with the sailboat just beyond when Good Boy tells Calypso to pull in to land, so she cuts the engine and raises it to coast onto the beach. The boat hits the sand and the V-bow digs in, then the hull tips to the side a little. She looks at Good Boy and puts a hand on his collar.

He looks at her and nods.

"Stay in the boat and be ready in case we're being chased back," he says, and hops over the gunnel into the final shallow reaches of the waves with Juan Manuel right behind him. "And don't leave to pick up another Drunk Monkey!" Juan Manuel says.

"Don't call him that anymore. You said he doesn't like it." She says.

"It's the name you gave him!"

"I'm not calling him that anymore, either."

"Why not?"

"I have a new name for him. I'll explain if we see each other again."

"If?"

She gives a blink of finality. "If."

Juan Manuel nods solemnly and Calypso salutes him like she saw the people do on the tele thing and he nods and runs after Good Boy.

She inhales the air, picking up the mixed scent of several tasty trees. The boat turns to the side a bit as the waves come in, then swings back toward the water as they withdraw. Closing her eyes, Calypso imagines she's on a tree limb that's moving back and forth in the wind. A loud click breaks her meditation, followed by what sounds like the squawk of a strange bird from a small box next to her on the seat.

A man's voice comes on over it.

"Where the hell are you guys?" the voice demands. "The idea was you to get here *before* nightfall so we didn't have to unload delicate explosives in the dark!"

Calypso sniffs at the box. Smells like people. It squawks again and she pulls herself away and slaps it with her claws.

"Are you idiots there?" the box says again.

A short stick protrudes from the annoying box, so Calypso grasps it in her claw and drags it to the edge of the bench.

Up and over the gunnel, the squawk box goes into the water and she doesn't have to hear it anymore.

Good Boy and Juan Manuel approach the forest that lines the cove and climbs up the steep hill alongside the cliff overlooking the barge and the beach where the people are staging blasting equipment. About halfway up, the vegetation becomes very dense and Good Boy gets stopped about a dog length in. Sticks and vines pull at his fur as he drags himself back out on his stomach.

"We might have to go around and attack them from the beach level. I can't get in far enough," he says, looking up to see Juan Manuel chewing leaves. "You're eating now?"

"Yeah," Juan Manuel says through a mouthful. "I'm going to eat a pathway through to the edge."

Good Boy frowns and looks for an alternative, his eyes riding up the nearest tree. The trunk isn't too wide and the branches don't start until well above the offending brush. It should give him a good view of what's going on below. He looks back at Juan Manuel.

"That's going to take all night," he says.

"You have a better idea? You could help out, but no, you're a big scary dog, and you don't eat such things. Plants are yucky!"

"They are," Good Boy says, and leaps onto the tree, gripping it in a bear hug. Limbs wrapped tight around the trunk, he scoots himself up while Juan Manuel watches in amazement.

"You climb trees, too?" Juan Manuel asks.

"No. Why do you ask?"

"Because if that's not you, then there's a really ugly animal climbing the tree near me. Sort of looks like a dog, but worse."

Good Boy ignores him and looks to the bottom of the cliff. There are people moving on the barge and a small boat on the beach, plus more people and a bunch of people stuff. The air blows along the cliff face at him and he smells Shriya and Miguel among other people. And Zonda. He shimmies back down and shakes himself off.

"They're on the beach," Good Boy reports to his friend.

"Look, I've already cleared a path," Juan Manuel says proudly, "the thick vegetation doesn't go up that high."

"Good job. Remember where this is. I think if we can get Shriya's attention and get her to follow us back into the forest, we can race to the boat and get out of here."

"I hope so. The less violent the better, especially with people with guns," Juan Manuel says "Did you learn to climb trees from Calypso?"

"Did that look graceful like Calypso?" Good Boy asks. "No, the people taught me that in security school."

"Maybe not graceful, but pretty good. Never seen you do that before."

"It's not something I've had to do before."

"What else can you do?" Juan Manuel asks.

"Hopefully, save Shriya from a bunch of bad people."

"And Miguel."

"Yeah," Good Boy nods, "if we can."

"I'm not arguing with you about this again!"

"Then don't."

The two friends reach the top of the overgrown road near the ruins of the old fort and walk along the tree line to stay hidden from the full moon's illumination. Good Boy's ears turn forward and he stops dead. Juan Manuel looks carefully for danger, but doesn't see any. Shriya's car is ahead near the cliff's edge, facing out to the water. There's a dim light on inside it.

"Are you sure they're not in the car?" Juan Manuel asks.

"Yes. You hear that?"

Juan Manuel hears forest animals with a hint of people. "I hear a bunch of things."

"No," Good Boy says, "Listen. It's that annoying sound the car makes when the door is open. I was worried one of the bad people were in it, but I think it's empty. Let's take a look."

They approach the car cautiously and, sure enough, it's empty. Good Boy detects the scent of the bad people around the door. A cacophony of shouting people rises up from the beach, so Good Boy and Manuel go over to the edge of the cliff and look down. People are carrying boxes from a small, beached boat to what might be a cave below, or a space under the ledge.

"Do you think I could pee on them from up here?" Juan Manuel asks.

Good Boy looks back at the car. "It would probably get blown around by the wind and come back on us, but I know something that won't—you see those two sitting below us?"

"Yeah, those are the ones I'm talking about peeing on."

"Do you think I can get them with the car?"

"What?" Juan Manuel asks, "you climb one tree, so now you think you can drive?"

"I don't know if I can drive it or not, but I was thinking we could *push* it over the side."

Juan Manuel looks to the men below, then back at the car, then the men again.

"OK. Maybe," he says, "but then what?"

"I don't know, I just want to see if I could squash at least one of them."

"What if we need the car to escape?" Juan Manuel says. "If we manage to get them to follow us back up here, wouldn't it be faster to take . . . oh, we would still need to get Calypso."

"Right. Do you think you can climb this cliff down to the beach?"

"So you can drop the car on me?"

"No" Good Boy says, "after we drop the car!"

"I should be able to. Can you?"

"No, I'll have to take the forest."

Juan Manuel assesses the condition and placements of the ledges in the cliff wall. "Might take a while. Probably makes more sense to go with you through the forest. I don't know what good I'll be down there without you."

"I don't, either, I'm just trying to think about our options. Help me figure out how to get this thing over the cliff before they decide to move." Good Boy hops into the driver's seat and looks around. "I wish Calypso was here."

"She can drive a car?"

"No, but she's better with this kind of stuff."

Juan Manuel looks at the dashboard for a minute and says, "Isn't there a thing they turn behind the wheel to wake it up?"

Good Boy nods and looks around. He hits the turn indicator and the wiper stalks to no effect.

Juan Manuel shakes his head. "It's on the other side. I'm pretty sure it's small."

Good Boy sticks his nose through the spokes in the wheel and Juan Manuel presses himself inside to help, pushing Good Boy sideways, wrenching his snout between the spokes.

"Ow," Good Boy complains, "what are you doing?"

"Trying to help."

"Well, you broke my nose."

"Let me see."

Good Boy turns to him and Juan Manuel inspects his face side to side. "Were your nostrils always on one side like that?"

"Funny."

"You're fine. Get out and I'll see if I can find it."

Good Boy takes another look around the steering column and sees the key sticking out. "No, I need you to look out and make sure the bad guys are still below so we can squash them."

"OK."

Good Boy tries to hit the key with his paw, but that doesn't do anything. He leans out the door. "I don't think that works," he admits to Juan Manuel. "I tried hitting it, but nothing happened."

Juan Manuel stares at Good Boy while he thinks for a moment.

"You have to turn it!" Good Boy finally says .With a frown and some contortion of his head behind the wheel to get his teeth on the key, he's able to turn it. The car starts up, the wipers flap up and down the windshield, music comes on, and the dash lights up.

"Hey, I got it!" Good Boy says proudly.

"Yeah, good work!" Juan Manuel responds, suddenly right next to Good Boy inside the car, taking him by surprise.

"Are there any bad people down there?" Good Boy asks.

"Yeah, the same two, let's go!"

Good Boy jumps out and the car stays put. "Uh, what do we do?" he says. "Maybe you have to be inside it for it to go?"

Juan Manuel shakes his head. "We were just inside it and it didn't move."

They both get behind the car and try to push, but it's stuck in place. They attempt it a few more times before realizing they need to try something else.

"The back moves up a little bit, but not forward." Juan Manuel says, puzzled.

"Well, we're not trying to lift it up, so that's no help."

"How do the people make it go?"

"I have no idea," Good Boy admits. "It doesn't have a handle to move it like the boat. Maybe whatever makes it stop is holding it in place."

"It could . . . it *must* have something holding it, right?" Juan Manuel considers. "Otherwise, it would roll away like a ball."

Good Boy thinks about that for a moment. "Yeah, exactly." He catches a sudden and intense whiff of goat and looks at Juan Manuel.

"What?"

"Why do you stink so strongly all of a sudden?"

"That's not me, that's the other goats."

Good Boy looks behind him to see the herd of goats standing a distance away in the dark looking at them curiously.

"Perfect!" Good Boy exclaims. "They can help us push."

"Maybe, but I don't think that will work."

"What's your plan, then?"

"I don't know," Juan Manuel says. "I need to think through what the people do when they work the car."

"It's not the wheel because that turns it," Good Boy says.

"Right, like that big boat at the island with those unfriendly goats."

"They might have been unfriendly, but it was the sheep that were the problem."

"Yeah, but I expect better from goats."

"What about *these* goats?" Good Boy asks.

"These goats are good." Juan Manuel turns to the herd and calls them. A few come over and the rest follow behind, but stay back a little.

Good Boy snorts. "I don't think we can fit enough of them back here to push this thing."

"That's why I think we need to figure out how it works." Juan Manuel goes halfway inside the car and tries to remember what the people do. They get it running . . . then they put on the strap thing . . . He finds the seatbelt hanging from the B-pillar and pulls it over to the other side of the seat. He lets it go and it retracts, which he finds frustrating.

"I don't think that does it," Good Boy says, squeezing himself next to him.

145

"Obviously."

"No, I mean even if you got it to stay pulled out."

"Well," Juan Manuel says, "what's your idea?"

"Shriya gets in, wakes it up, pulls that strap thing, then . . . what does she do?"

"If I knew, I'd do it."

"I know that," Good Boy almost snaps. "I'm not asking you."

"Then who are you asking?"

"Myself."

Juan Manuel is about to make a joke, but his good horn catches on the headliner. "Ah!" He pulls his horn down and it tears the headliner so that tatters of it hang above the seat. The still-moving wiper blades appear to mock him. "How do you turn those flapping arms off?—they're driving me nuts!" He flips a steering column control stalk with his nose and the wipers stop. "Ha! I did it."

"That's it," Good Boy barks excitedly. "That's the stick!"

"That only does the arms."

"No, the one between the seats." Good Boy pushes Juan Manuel aside and climbs over the seat to grab the shifter with his teeth.

"I can't get it to move," he mumbles.

"Let me take a look at it."

"Hold on." Good Boy looks at it carefully and notices a button on the side. He grabs it in his mouth again, but this time bites the button and the stick awkwardly shifts back and stops. The car starts to roll forward and he scrambles to get out, but his leg catches in the seatbelt. Juan Manuel grabs his uninjured back leg, but the car keeps rolling. With a lucky guess, Good Boy twists the right way to untangle himself and escape and he and Juan Manuel look at each other and smile as the front wheels fall off the edge. The car slides to a halt, the front wheels spinning a few times in the air before running out of momentum.

Good Boy blinks at the car in resignation. "Now what?"

"Push?"

"Yeah, maybe now it will work."

With a little shove from some of the herd goats, the underside of the car slides on the grass and the back flips up in the air as it disappears over the side. It makes a quick series of thuds and bangs before there's a tremendous crash that ends with the angry shouts of people.

Good Boy and Juan Manuel rush to the side to look down. A light still blinks on and off from the car, shining on the ledges of the cliff wall. People are pointing up at them and there's a flash of a gun. Soil and stone becomes a puff of dust in front of Juan Manuel as the rapport from the rifle echoes back and forth within the cove and bullets zip by them in the air. They see three men run for the jungle side of the beach just as they step out of the line of fire.

"What about Calypso?" Juan Manuel asks.

"She'll be fine where she is—they're coming for us!"

"You think we got them?" Juan Manuel asks.

"I don't know, people tend to get unreasonably angry when it comes to cars being damaged, so that will surely make them mad on its own."

"You think Shriya's going to notice that I ripped the roof with my horn."

"Pretty sure she'll be more angry about what the cliff and beach did to the rest of it."

"That's true—she'll be more mad at them! Now what?"

"We drew some of them up the path leading this way," Good Boy says. "We need to get through the vegetation off the path and get to the beach for whoever is left and get Shriya without them hearing us."

Juan Manuel shakes his head and motions to the members of the herd who didn't run at the sound of the gunfire. "We can't. Even if we can sneak by them in the trees, what about these goats."

"Tell them they need to hide in the forest."

Two goats step forward. "We can help you," they say.

"You don't have to," Juan Manuel tells them. "The bad people are coming up here for us."

"We know, and they killed the shepherd."

Juan Manuel turns to Good Boy. "Maybe we can fight off these men if enough of them help."

Good Boy looks at the respectable number of remaining goats. "We need to fight these people," he tells Juan Manuel. "If we can throw at least one of them off the cliff, some more might follow and that could clear the beach of them enough for us to go down and get Shriya and Miguel."

"How are we going to do that?" Juan Manuel asks.

"The way we always do—let them underestimate us. People don't see as well as we do in the dark," Good Boy says. "If we use the forest as cover, I don't think they'll know what's happening. With enough help from the goats, they won't know what to do when we go in and out of the forest."

"The problem is if they get too far from the trees, they'll be able to get us with their guns," Juan Manuel says.

"We'll have to hit them right away, then," Good Boy says.

"I agree, but the tree cover doesn't go to the cliff. So we might not be able to get them close enough to the cliff to push them off and we'll be in the open."

"What are you thinking?"

"These goats can block the people from getting too far into the open," Juan Manuel says. "Also, like you said that they underestimate us. People don't think goats are dangerous—they herd us around, eat us, cut pieces of us off—what if we herd *them*? Herd them right off the cliff."

"They'll shoot back," Good Boy says.

"If we act like we're dumb, I think we can get them close enough and then charge them quickly. If we get it right, they won't be able to shoot many times. We have enough numbers."

"Might be bloody."

"Probably," Juan Manuel agrees.

"We're going to need to convince them to risk their lives for strangers."

Juan Manuel turns to the herd. "Fellow goats, we need your help against the people."

"We can't beat men with guns," one of them bleats.

"Together we can! This dog is Good Boy—taught by the men to be a man-killer—and he and I have beaten people with guns before."

"Then why do you need us?" another asks.

"Because there's more of them than we've beaten at one time."

"Some of us might be killed."

"Probably," Juan Manuel says, "but these men coming up are the ones who killed your shepherd."

"If we stay out of it, we'll all live," says another.

One of the braver goats blows a raspberry at them for their cowardice and walks up to stand next to Juan Manuel, who nods.

"Yes, you might live," Juan Manuel takes a dramatic breath, "until some other person rounds you up, and who knows what kind of person that will be? Maybe he will be someone who eats goats."

Some of the goats murmur with worry.

"The man being held by the bad people down there on the beach is a shepherd and he is a good person. His herd is friendly and fun and he doesn't eat them. He takes us where we are free to roam and eat as we please and I'm certain that he would take all of you in, but he needs your help."

The goats don't respond with the vigor Juan Manuel was hoping for, so he looks over the herd and shouts. "What kind of life do you want to live? Do you want to live your life in wait to see what the people will do with you, or go into the rainforest to risk yourselves against the jaguars, or do you want to act with the stubborn bravery that we are known for? Do you want to stand up to bad people and stand up for friends?"

The response is subdued, but more encouraging. Juan Manuel pushes harder. "Sheep give in and sheep don't have horns, but we do!"

149

"*We* don't!" one of the goats heckles him.

"Only because they were removed, but I don't mean actual horns, I mean the horns inside of you! Sheep don't have that!"

"What about rams?" another one asks with a snicker.

Good Boy chuckles.

"Forget rams! Do you know how I lost half of this horn?" Juan Manuel lets his gaze take in all of them. "I lost it to a gun while chasing after these same bad men. I got shot, but I am still here, still fighting because that's what we do! Are we sheep or are we goats?"

Juan Manuel smiles as the herd calls back with more enthusiasm. "While the ordinary goats living ordinary lives of sheepish resignation, butting each other for pretend control over a piece of land the people have fenced them onto," he cries out to them, "those of us who survive today will know true courage and we will look in the water for the rest of our days and know that the rippling face staring back is the face of a goat of true bravery!"

Most of the goats bleat in unison of agreement with the few holdouts joining in to not be left out. Good enough, Juan Manuel thinks, nodding and smiling.

Good Boy looks at him with admiration. "That'll do, goat. That'll do."

"It better," Juan Manuel whispers to him, "or I'm going to be responsible for any of these goats that get killed for nothing."

"Win or lose, it won't be for nothing."

The herd gathers around. "What's the plan?" one of them asks.

Good Boy nods. "OK, we don't have much time. Here's the plan . . ."

Three pirates reach the edge of the forest at the top of the cliff and scan for people, but they only see goats eating the foliage around the bottoms of the trees, leaving a path open along the edge of the cliff. Good Boy and Juan Manuel watch them from the darkness across the path. The first man walks quietly into the open in a crouch and the herd of goats start to move a little toward him.

"They're going to give it away too soon," Good Boy says with worry. The second man follows and most of the herd walks conspicuously at the two men.

Juan Manuel bleats a warning to the herd to wait, prompting the third man to point a gun in his general direction.

"Don't move!" Good Boy warns. "Their eyes work on movement in the dark. If you stay still, they can't see us."

Juan Manuel stays perfectly still as the man's gun scans past him and down the path before following the other two men into a huddle to discuss what to do next. The herd subtly closes up in a loose circle around the men, prompting the last man to point to them.

"These goats are creeping me out, man," he says. "Maybe they pushed the car over the cliff."

"Yeah, they're mad we killed their shepherd," says a man with a sparkly earring and a bandana over his head.

"You think so?"

"No! They're goats. Animals are dumb, they don't think, they just react by instinct."

Two of the men point their guns at the herd and two goats run away. The remaining two dozen keep idly chewing.

"See?" the man with the earring laughs, hitting the third man on the shoulder. "Come on, eh! Are you afraid of some goats?"

"What about that sloth that drives the boat?" the third man asks.

"You believe that story?" Earring asks and he and the second man laugh. "Mateo was messing with you, man!"

"He didn't sound like he was joking."

"Ask yourself how that can be true."

"Pablo's ghost."

Giving up, Earring shakes his head and leads them farther onto the grounds of the fort. Good Boy and Juan Manuel quietly slip from cover to follow. The men are lit up by the moon, moving away from the edge.

"We need to go now!" Good Boy shouts and Juan Manuel bleats the command to charge. The goats all bleat war cries and rush the men, who swing their rifles at them. Good Boy overtakes a goat and launches off his back to tackle the closest man to the ground as the herd overwhelms them. A rifle goes off with a double bang, but hits nothing. The other two men run back for the path to the beach, but are blocked by charging goats who had been waiting in the forest. Now the men are trapped near the cliff. Good Boy lets the third man up and he limps over without his rifle to the others being pressed closer to the edge.

"I told you!" he yells. "They're trying to drive us off the side!".

"It's impossible!"

"No, it's happening!" the other shouts. Two of the men lift their rifles and the goats rush the remaining distance. One lunges at Earring, who ducks to his left. The goat falls onto his side to try to stop, but slips and slides off the ledge, disappearing into the dark.

Earring has no time to celebrate before another goat slams into him with a rib-breaking hit to his side. With flailing arms and a scream of terror, he trips over the edge. The remaining man with a gun gets off another shot, but hits nothing as a goat rears up and shoves him over. Grasping for a handhold, he catches the third man's arm and they fall to their deaths together.

The remaining herd gathers around the threshold of the pirates' oblivion, but they can't see where they hit the ground. Men shout from the beach and Good Boy spots them raising guns in their direction. One of them shouts, "It's that dog!"

Good Boy orders everyone away from the edge as bullets chip and ricochet off the ledge and zip by his head. As the echo dies down, a lone goat bleats quietly from below the cliff. Good Boy crawls over on his belly and peeks over the edge. The goat that had gone over the side has landed on a ledge just below him. The gunmen are shouting to each other, but not looking up. He sticks his head fully over the side and calls down to the goat.

"Are you hurt?"

The goat does a quick self-assessment and looks up. "No."

"Can you get back up . . ." Good Boy looks along the cliff, but doesn't see any way up, "somehow?"

"No, there's not enough ledge."

"Can you get down to the beach?"

The goat looks down and plots a route from ledge to ledge. "Yes, but that's where the people are."

"That's where we're going next. If you head down, we can meet you there."

"I'll get down there faster than you."

"They won't be expecting an attack from the cliff," Good Boy says, "so wait for us to raid the beach and look for an opening to take them by surprise."

The goat nods. "You're as smart as the people."

"No, but they trained me."

The goat looks down at the pirates pointing guns at two other people and making them drag the fallen bodies to the middle of the beach.

"Are those your friends?" he asks, turning back to Good Boy, but he's already gone. Looking back down at the last of the cliff-divers being laid out on the sand, the people don't look so menacing—fragile even. Without their guns, they're not so invincible.

As Good Boy leads the herd down the hillside forest off of the path, the nimble goats have to hold back to avoid getting ahead of him. They hear people yelling from the beach and a boat motoring away. A dog barks and Good Boy stops to listen.

It's Zonda.

He takes a deep breath and hopes he doesn't have to fight her. Out of the corner of his eye, he sees Juan Manuel staring at him, so he turns his way.

153

"Is that Zonda?" Juan Manuel asks.

Good Boy looks away and tries to think of something funny, but he can't. "Yes," he answers quietly.

"If we have to fight her, I can do it."

"Thanks, but she's not a dumb street dog."

"There *were* three of them," Juan Manuel says.

"And you were losing."

"Yeah, well, if there were only two of them, they'd have been crawling back home like worms." Good Boy looks at him as if waiting for a better punchline and Juan Manuel frowns, "You know, because all their bones would have been broken."

"Well, I'm not doubting you, but Zonda's even more than three street dogs," Good Boys says. "I don't even know if I can beat her."

"You're bigger than her."

"She's faster."

"How do you know?"

"I trained with dogs like her."

"I thought you were the same kind of dog."

"No, we just sort of look alike."

The group moves quietly down the rest of the way to the tree line at the edge of the beach and forms into lines three goats deep that are separated by trees. Juan Manuel and Good Boy can see what looks like Shriya and Miguel being held in a seated position against the fallen beach tree trunk by two men with guns at the far end. Another man behind them is tying their arms behind their backs. Two more stand a short way from them, arguing loudly while another pees on the wall.

One of the arguing men yells that they're dealing with a dog and he can't reason with a dog while the other tells him he's crazy and that some other people must be up there, though Good Boy doesn't understand all of the words. The small boat and the bodies of the men that were driven off the cliff are lined up neatly along its bottom. Shriya's car is on its roof, door broken off, front compacted and bent. Somehow, music still plays from it.

Zonda comes to attention with a gruff bark of warning and looks to the forest, freezing Good Boy's blood, but that only helps with the heat.

Juan Manuel stands at the front of the line next to Good Boy and nods. "I've got your back in case she runs circles around you and tries to attack you from behind. I'll let her chew on me a bit until you turn around."

Good Boy grunts a laugh. "Whatever happens to me, get yourself and Shriya back to Calypso. If I don't make it off the beach, I'll be fine if one of the people who killed the Man dies with me. But to do that, I need to get by Zonda."

"You and I took on Thundersloth and a large pack of spear-wielding chimpanzees!" Juan Manuel says. "These are only a few people, and we have a herd of brave goats."

The small boat motors onto the opposite end of the beach and another man jumps off the bow. Two of the others help him pull the boat higher onto the sand.

"And now there's another one," Good Boy says, "and they all have guns."

"And the rest are stuck on the small land. We have an angry herd that's tired of waiting to see what people will decide to do to us and we're not gonna take it anymore! They can't shoot us all!" Juan Manuel is about to leap onto the beach, but Good Boy presses his nose to his shoulder to stop him.

"Hold on, battle goat. You can't go rushing at them or they'll shoot half of you down before the ones in back can clear the tree line."

"We need to close the distance as quickly as possible to overwhelm them," Juan Manual insists.

"That's a good way to get most of the herd killed. Anger can be a motivator, but it isn't a planner," Good Boy coaches him. "The people are so powerful because they learned to think over their feelings."

Juan Manuel stomps and blows out his hurt pride with a snort. "Fine, but they think much better than we can."

"That's why we need to be the ones to think and we need to keep them from doing so. We kept them confused and afraid when we saved you from being eaten and we did that now to drive them off the cliff."

"Then what should we do?"

"Wander onto the beach," Good Boy says, "kind of slow, like you all came down here aimlessly."

"We'll be easier targets than a sloth!"

"Exactly. How do sloths survive so well?"

"I thought we concluded that they must taste bad, so—"

"We don't have time for jokes." Good Boy growls.

"I don't know," Juan Manuel frowns, "they're good at not being seen and live far up in trees where few things can get them."

"OK, I was looking more for the first one."

"I don't understand—they'll definitely see us on the beach."

"Right, but sloths don't really hide, so much as they look like part of a tree, understand?" Good Boy says.

"We need to look like something else."

"Right, and what about Calypso?"

"What do you mean?" Juan Manuel asks. "She's a sloth, so it's the same thing."

"Yes, but she's done stuff sloths shouldn't be able to do, that sloths *don't* do. She's slow, but time and again has taken dangerous enemies by surprise because none of them expect any of that from someone so unthreatening," Good Boy eyes his friend, and then the herd of goats. "Have anything we've encountered ever been frightened of her?"

"No." Juan Manuel narrows his eyes at the bad people. "They underestimated her."

"Yes! And the people underestimate goats, too. You said it—to them you're harmless, walking food," Good Boy grins and all his teeth show menacingly. "So wander out there a few at a time, make some noise, act goofy, don't look like you care about the people, have the ones in the front get close to them as the

156

ones in the back kind of crowd the beach—look like you all got lose from the pen since they killed the shepherd and now you're going for a stroll and checking things out curiously."

"Then, when we're close enough, we attack!" Juan Manuel nods.

"Exactly. You'll be on your own until then, since I won't be able to go with you. If Zonda sees or smells me, she'll attack, so I'll wait here for you, then I'll race along the water to the far end of the beach to get to Shriya, flank the enemy while they're fighting with the herd, or," he looks away and sighs, "take on Zonda."

"I feel good about this."

"Don't feel—think!"

"That's something I'd never expect to hear from a dog."

"I'm how the people made me."

Juan Manuel nods. "So, when do we do it?"

"What's wrong with now?"

Juan Manuel smiles and turns to the herd.

"This dog was trained to fight by the people and he has a good plan," he tells them. "We all wander onto the beach a bit separately and act like we're looking for food and are curious about what's going on. Some of us should move toward the water, maybe someone can go look at the crushed car, get creative! What would you do if the people weren't there? When we can manage to get at least one of each of us near the people, we attack at the same time and the rest rush to help."

"Watch out for the dog," Good Boy warns. "She was trained like I was. The people are arrogant, but she won't be as easily fooled. To keep them all from getting suspicious, I have to stay hidden until the attack. You'll be dealing with her until I can get there. I suggest no less than three of you on her. OK?" He looks around the herd and they nod their understanding.

"Tonight, we aren't goats and a dog, we are all one pack." Good Boy looks at Juan Manuel, who nods and steps onto the sand followed by two other goats. The rest slowly filter out of the trees and onto the beach.

Zonda barks to get the attention of the people, but they just glance curiously at the goats and go back to talking. Zonda barks louder and pulls on her leash, but Rico kicks her in the side and commands her to shut up.

Juan Manuel realizes she will probably recognize him, so he decides to head right for her and feign being friendly.

"Where are all these goats coming from?" one of the men asks.

"We killed their shepherd," another says and spits into the sand. "They probably got free and wandered down here."

"I don't know, maybe they're the ones who pushed the car off the cliff and killed Taco and Bacca and Nando and now they are coming for us!"

All the men laugh except for Rico. "Laugh it up," he says, "but someone's up there and they have the high ground. They must not have the numbers or they'd be taking advantage."

"It's these goats!"

Rico glares at him. "Say that one more time and I'm sending you up there alone to see who's up there. Those idiots aren't back with the rest of the explosives yet and aren't answering their walkie talkie. Something is going on and you think it's goats?"

"These two must have told someone else."

"Or Rondo has other friends," another offers.

"We can rough these up some more."

"No, they might be the only reason whoever is up there isn't taking advantage of the situation."

"Other than dropping a car on us."

"Baahaahaahaahaa," one of the goats bleats in a friendly manner to one of the men.

The man laughs and pets the goat's head. "Look at this," he says, "maybe these goats didn't like their shepherd and they're thanking us, huh?"

More goats form up in a circle around the men. Zonda intimidates them out of the reach of her leash.

"Zonda! Down!" the man yanks hard on her leash and hits her shoulder.

Juan Manuel bleats at the man and steps closer to Zonda.

"Hey, are you OK?" he asks.

"I'm fine," she snarls at him.

"He hits you?"

"He's a person. They're all like that."

"No, they're not. Just the bad ones."

"He's not bad."

"How do you explain closing people into a cave or killing other people or hitting you?"

"It's the way of the world."

"It doesn't have to be."

"Where's your friend and the . . . sloth, is it?"

"They headed back to the town."

"Did they?" she asks suspiciously.

"Hey!" one of the men shouts, pointing at Juan Manuel. "That's the goat with the broken horn that was with them!"

Rico does a double take and Juan Manuel bleats as loud as he can. The goats all rear up on their back legs and attack. With the first hits to the spines and abdomens of the men, the rest of the goats rush from the forest into the fight and Good Boy launches out of the shadows down the dense wet sand at the sea's edge in a race to get to Shriya.

Vicious sounds from Zonda and cries from the goats assail his ears as he passes the fight, unable to help. Leaping a large driftwood log, Good Boy catches the neck of the man guarding Shriya and Miguel and uses it to pivot himself through the air, bringing the man to the sand, and leaving him hopelessly clutching his throat.

"Buca!" Shriya exclaims.

No hesitation, Good Boy attacks the heavy zip tie that binds Shriya's hands behind her back, his teeth ripping through them with ease before freeing her legs in the same fashion. Miguel is next and his hands are free when gunshots go off and some goats cry out.

Over the log again, leaving Miguel's feet to himself, Good Boy finds Zonda has driven off a number of the goats and the pirates are cutting them down with rifles. Two pirates lay on the ground unmoving while Juan Manuel and another goat struggle to keep the rest from aiming properly at the fleeing herd.

None of the men is the one Good Boy is looking for, which only makes him angrier. With a double leap, he pushes off Juan Manuel with his back legs and catches another pirate by the neck with his lethal spinning take down. Landing on all fours, Good Boy attacks the crotch of the next closest pirate and two of the remaining goats crash into that man's head from each side, dropping him with a thump like a heavy bag of dog food.

One of the goats goes down from a bullet from two pirates crouching alone at the base of the cliff. Good Boy gathers Juan Manuel and calls on the goats to charge when the goat from the cliff drops onto the men from a ledge high above. Scrambling to his feet, the heavy goat stomps them until they no longer move.

"Whoa, where did he come from?" Juan Manuel asks.

"He went over the side when we were fighting up top," Good Boy pants. "I forgot all about him."

"I saw him go over! I thought he was dead." Juan Manuel spots a pirate fighting off two goats using his rifle like a club and he rushes into the fight.

Rico notices the danger he's in and calls out to Zonda as he tries to get some distance from Good Boy to shoot him. A rifle from one of the downed pirates sits on the sand. Good Boy grabs the shoulder strap in his teeth and drags it to Shriya. She snatches it and ducks behind the log as the pirate takes a shot at her. The bullet embeds itself in the thick driftwood, sending shivers of wood through the air.

Ending her pursuit of the goats, Zonda turns and rushes for Good Boy. Some of the goats in the forest call out to the others that she is no longer chasing them and most of them stop and charge back into the fray. Horizontal streaks of light and a rapid banging echoes off the walls, pounding within their skulls as a machine gun on the barge is brought to bear on the beach.

Three running goats immediately trip into the sand with heavy thuds, their bodies twisted into unnatural poses. Zonda and Rico run for the crashed car to take whatever cover it might provide while Good Boy, Juan Manuel, and a goat friend jump the massive log and try to melt themselves into the backside of it for protection. Next to them, Shriya and Miguel desperately press themselves into the sand behind the log.

Bullets thud into the beach, pound into the wood, tear into it, blow off chunks, and smash through the thinner sections near the top. The machine gun moves on to the cliff face, showering the friends with shards of rock. From all over the beach, goats cry out in pain and fear, some running in circles of confusion. The moment seems to last forever, the terrible pounding of mechanized death and the bleating of goats being cut down seem to take over the entirety of the universe and, unable to take it all, Juan Manuel adds his own screams to the mix.

Good Boy wants to bite his friend to draw him back into the fight, but he knows that won't work and that there's nothing they can do against the horrifying power of the people's technology. All he can do is try to endure until there's an opportunity to get the survivors off the beach.

The gun goes silent and Good Boy is about to go over the top when a pirate on the other side of the log shouts curses at the barge. He is soon cut short by renewed fire from his own comrades. The pirate drops onto the wood with a thump heavy with finality. Blood drools from the man's open mouth, his lifeless eyes staring accusingly.

Good Boy realizes too late that he has underestimated the people and led everyone to their death. "I didn't know! I didn't know!" he yells to his friend, but Juan Manuel's eyes don't register anything but terror.

Charge of the Slow Foot

Calypso hears the rapid percussion overlaying a cacophony of goats bleating in fear. Light flashes across the water from somewhere behind the trees growing on the headland that extends into the sea between her beach and the one where her friends were headed. In the boat, an incongruously upbeat song comes on with brass instruments. A man sings to someone to hold on, he's coming.

Calypso blinks at the strange flashing. A distant dog barks with a fear Calypso hasn't heard since Pablo was killed, and her blood runs cold as she realizes the flashing must be some kind of terrible gun. It strikes her that if she waits here much longer, there will be no one to wait for!

The stern of the boat rises up on an incoming wave. Without looking, Calypso pushes the stick forward to lower the motor and starts it. Another wave raises the boat again. The drive clunks into reverse and she pulls the go handle all the way back. The bow holds onto the sand for a moment before the motor drags it reluctantly up another incoming wave that collides with the transom, breaking up to wash over the gunwales and canopy.

Merely paused by the force of the surf, the raging motor fights the boat through. Past the breakers, Calypso turns the stick to aim the boat for the flashing lights. A large wave hits abeam and she has to grab tight onto the stick and the seat to keep from being thrown to the side of the boat.

Clunk!

She shifts the boat into forward gear and rides over the next wave. Jamming the throttle forward, the motor revs up, the prop spins up, slipping, churning the water. The boat accelerates as the blades grip the water, but the front is still reluctant to rise. Playing the stick forward and back as she feels the boat ride over the waves, Calypso is able to coax the hull up on plane in spite of the strangely heavy bow, and it takes all her concentration to hold the boat at speed while aiming it at the noise and flashing light.

On the floating platform, Rondo screams and tries to fight his way out of the grasp of the pirates, but they hold him fast. Empty shells and links from the ammunition belt clatter to the deck and tracer bullets stream towards the shore with four dark bullets unseen between each flashing streak. Medium sized animals are running in terror, but the tracers follow, turning the ones it catches into unmoving lumps on the sand.

Click!

From the bleating coming from the beach, Rondo now realizes that the slaughtered animals are goats. He immediately thinks of Charleston and the wave of fear he has for Shriya becomes a tsunami of defiance, rage surging through him, driving him to no longer sit in resignation. Looking for something sharp to cut the zip ties securing his hands behind his back, his eyes fall upon a large accretion of sand and treasure that had been brought up from the wreck site sitting on the deck not even a meter away. Protruding from the layers is the arm of a silver crucifix. Nobody is watching him, so he slides over while they're distracted.

The gunner grins ghoulishly as he reloads the ammo. One of their own shouts angrily from the beach. Pulling the charging handle, the gunner turns to the guy next to him and sneers, "Less to share with!"

"What kind of men are overtaken by a bunch of goats?" the other pirate laughs. Are they men or little kittens?" The gunner opens fire again.

Over the partial deafness caused by the gun fire, one of the men holding Rondo somehow hears the sound of a straining boat motor coming towards them. "There's our explosives, finally!" he yells, pointing.

A second pirate with blurred old tattoos on his neck steps forward, brow wrinkled nervously, suspicious. "Where the hell have they been? Why didn't they respond?"

The first pirate picks up the two-way radio and tries to call the Speedwell, but just gets static. He pulls out his satellite phone and sees that he has a message from one of the men who were bringing the explosives.

The gunner sees the phone and stops firing to try to knock it from his hand, but misses as the man yanks his hand away.

"I said no phones!"

"The radio isn't working, and there's a message from Esteban!" Standing out of the gunner's reach, he calls him back. "Esteban!" he greets and listens gravely. "Yes, the boat is heading to us now." His face turns pale, "Is it the Evolution Movement?"

"Evo! Why would they be after us?" The neck tattoo pirate asks nervously.

"Pablo was one of them," the gunner says with a shrug. "They aren't what they used to be. If they come for us, we kill them, too."

"*Who* stole the boat?!" The man on the phone yells. A moment later, he lowers the phone and stares at the Speedwell as if it were a ghost, then grabs the gunner's arm before he can resume firing. "The animals stole the boat!"

"How is that possible?!" The gunner howls in rage.

"It was the dog and the sloth!" another pirate yells nervously.

The man on the phone raises it back to his ear. "You had better have a good excuse for how some dumb animals stole the boat filled with the explosives we need to recover hundreds of millions of dollars in treasure! Are you men, what are you?!"

"They are not only animals," the nervous pirate interrupts, "it is Pablo's ghost! I told you before—"

"Mateo, shut up with that nonsense!"

"You are the nonsense! The beach is being attacked by goats and a dog! That is Pablo's possessed demon sloth driving his old boat coming for revenge, you sonofabitch!"

The gunner turns, looking to punch him, but the man on the phone puts his hand on his shoulder. "Esteban says a goat got

164

into the truck and they all tried to get him out without knocking over any of the explosives, then he suddenly hopped out and ran to the boat and away they went. He didn't see a sloth, but there was a dog with them."

"What kind of dog?" Mateo asks.

The man on the phone repeats the question to Esteban. A moment later, he holds the phone away from his ear and stares at the gunner with an incredulous look. "It was a German Shepherd."

Ashen-faced, the gunner returns to the machine gun and trains it on the Speedwell.

Mateo points at the gunner, "See?! We are all—"

"Ghost or not, that boat is real! Watch me blow it out of the water."

As Calypso thought, the rapid banging, flashing lights streaking into the beach must be from a more terrible kind of gun than they've ever encountered before. On shore, shadowy figures run in disarray. The streaks of light trace their movements and even between the lightning, the figures drop to the ground, one by one.

Driven by fear for her friends and a kind of anger she has never known before, Calypso tries to push the go handle past its limit. No more, yet why is it so slow?! This isn't the time for the boat to be lazy! Adjusting the stick, she levels the boat and picks up a bit more speed off the backside of a wave in her rush towards the gun.

The flash and noise stops and she gains valuable distance, wondering what happened. Closing in to where she thinks she needs to start making her move, Calypso's eyes are suddenly dazzled by strobing flashes that turn to burning lines zipping over the top of the boat and alongside, each streak of light sending up several splashes of water.

It stops for a moment and there's some kind of movement on the barge. A slow blink later and the outline of the barge has gotten closer. The gun flashes again. The water splashes around the Speedwell and the hull cracks around her like the breaking of large tree limbs in a storm. Shivers of fear threaten to freeze Calypso in place and she has to force her muscles to action—to do anything at all—to keep them ready.

In an instant, the mocking monkeys, the pity of fast animals, the questions about how sloths can possibly survive, all reel through her mind until they stop dead with Zonda and Good Boy voices echoing: *Is the sloth a great warrior? You'd be surprised.* Now the barge is coming up quick and the boat shudders and vibrates as it absorbs fire, but Calypso is calm—everything is clear with the gun no longer firing on her friends. She takes in the power of the motor's thrust, the gentle wind that swirls around the sides of the windshield to run like gentle claws through her fur, the final smells of trees and ocean, even if ruined by the acrid cordite from the gun.

Crack-crack-crack-crack-crack!

The view through the windshield all but fractures into obscurity, lights dance in its sudden spider web cracks, the boat comes down off a wave, and chunks of the thick glass like sharp stones fall over the dashboard and onto the seat, drumming like massive raindrops onto the floor. Something zips through the seat beside Calypso and whacks into the back of the boat. Wind whistles through the shattered glass like a storm and dries her eyes. The smelly juice the boat drinks has suddenly become strong, overpowering the other smells. The gunfire stops. Men shout from the barge, their voices angry and inscrutable under the hiss of the wind and the pounding of the hull through the waves as the determined engine pushes it toward the barge.

Listening to the pirate's conversation in disbelief, Rondo realizes that it's the animals that had saved them in the ancient city attempting to do it again. He can't imagine how they got here and what they're going to do, but there's no way they can stand up to a machine gun. His wrists pop free as the edge of the crucifix breaks the zip tie. Fear disappears, concern for his future, the treasure, all of it forgotten as Rondo's heart pounds adrenaline, giving him a strength he never knew he had. The pirate fires warning shots around the speedboat and the cacophony of igniting powder and machine clatter drowns out the sound of Rondo bringing down the massive block of encrusted silver coins onto the head of the closest guy, the weight of it pulling him toward the deck on top of him.

Rondo lifts his head—the Speedwell is still coming. Another man pulls up a pistol, but Rondo jumps on him and they fall to the deck in a heap. The pirate gets his finger on the trigger and fires. Rondo shifts his elbow and jams the barrel into the man's hip as he fires again. The man screams and grabs his leg and Rondo takes his gun and stands up to continue the fight, but he's dizzy.

He slips on the wet floor of the boat and falls to his side, dropping the gun somewhere out of sight. Looking down at himself, he sees that the water is blood and some of it is his. Must be the adrenaline because he can't even feel it. The blood is coming from . . . looks like his pancreas. Putting some pressure on the wound, he becomes aware of what's going on around him. That monster he employed is firing on the impossible little sloth in the speedboat. Summoning all the defiance he can gather, he finds the strength to get to his feet. His vision is a black tunnel with the sides closing in as he lunges in the direction of the gunner.

"*Calypsooooo*!" he screams.

The gun firing on the shore stops and starts again, blasting out to sea. From the marginal safety of the small space between the cliff wall and the crumpled front of Shriya's smashed and bullet-torn car, Zonda shakes off sand and pulls at Rico to get him to climb out and continue the fight.

When he doesn't move, she smells the blood and realizes he has been hit. With a whimper that is quickly replaced by rage, she steps out from behind the car and surveys the once peaceful beach now littered with corpses of men and goats, the machine gun on the barge cracking death at a small boat that refuses to

167

turn away even as bullets pound into it, drawing it away from her and everyone around her. The bravery of the suicidal charge solidifies Zonda's resolve to fight to the end.

Shriya readies the gun in her hands and gets into a position where she can quickly come up and fire from behind the log. A remaining pirate yells for them to surrender and a goat from the herd hops up from where he had been playing dead to run for the water. The pirate whips the gun in its direction at the sound before seeing a fleeing goat and continuing his advance on the log.

Breathing hard, emanating heat and rage, muscles tensed, Good Boy hears sand hitting the side of the log from the pirate's approach and he knows he's in range. Releasing with a snap, twisting to his feet, in one fluid move he leaps onto the top of the splintered log, adjusts his aim, and launches himself to catch the pirate by the throat, but is intercepted by Zonda launching for his own neck and is thrown into a spin that ends with him crashing and rolling onto the sand.

Miguel aims a reclaimed rifle toward the machine gunner on the barge and Shriya lifts a rifle with a war cry of her own, firing up into the looming pirate, hopping back on her bottom to avoid the pirate falling over the log, and shifting the barrel over the log to try to get a shot on Zonda as she fights with Good Boy.

The barge explodes in a blinding light and a shockwave blows everyone over, reflecting off the walls and leaving behind a muffled world. The few remaining goats run for the cover of the trees. Shaken to his senses, Juan Manuel leaps the log and tries to rally them back, but they don't seem to hear him. Something moves with threatening quickness behind him and he instinctively kicks back, then whips his head around. His broken horn catches on a man's face and spins him to the ground.

Glancing at the man to see that he was a pirate and that he's now no longer a threat, the sudden realization of what happened to the barge sends Juan Manuel into a panic. He rushes for the shore, a desperate, screaming, bleat from the bottom of his soul accompanied by a psychic call like a concussive pulse into the heads of all the nearby animals.

"*Ca-lyp-so*!" he screams.

Good Boy jumps up from the sand in time to shake his head alert and avoid Zonda's teeth before slashing back defensively. The two dogs square off in a snarling twirling confrontation, looking for an opening in the other's stance.

Juan Manuel's heartbreaking lament continues behind them and he leaps into the surf. The waves are too great and they push him back to the beach. Catching a glimpse of Juan Manuel and realizing that their sloth friend must have crashed the boat into the barge to save them all from that terrible gun, Zonda puts away her fangs and backs off a step.

Good Boy turns to see Shriya standing behind them swing her gun away from Zonda to finish off the dazed pirate that had been hit by Juan Manuel as he attempts to stand up.

"Miguel, watch the beach!" Shriya shouts, hoping he hears, as she drops the rifle and runs for the shoreline, leaving her shirt in her wake. Zonda launches after her and Good Boy leaps off his weary legs, tearing away at full power to stop her before she gets to Shriya and Juan Manuel. Lungs pounding air, hot and heavy, sand scratching his eyes, fear like he's never had before drives Good Boy to run faster than he ever has even as Zonda continues pulling away.

She's almost on Shriya who has stopped to remove her shoes, unaware of the deadly ground eagle racing for them. Good Boy's barks fall on deaf ears and he's still three dog-lengths behind when Zonda crouches to jump . . .

. . . and continues past Shriya and into the surf, paddling up a cresting wave that flips her over back onto the beach. Juan Manuel yells again for Calypso and Good Boy's heart jolts with the realization of what has happened.

Zonda stands back up and tries swimming again. Good Boy leaps past her and over the top of a rolling wave. The salt stings his eyes and wounds, but the cool water returns some lost energy that he immediately puts to use paddling for the burning pieces of the barge. Floating debris bumps into him as he swims, the smell of burning wood and fiberglass filling his nose. The partial body of a person floats close by, smelling of burned meat and getting in his way of smelling for Calypso.

"Where are you going?" Miguel yells to Shriya, running toward the water after her.

"Calypso's out there!" Shriya screams. "Sloths float!"

"She would have been killed by the explosion!"

"No, she's out there!"

Miguel catches up to her as she hops out of her pants. "How is that possible?!" he asks.

"I don't know! Juan Manuel saw!"

"What?!"Miguel tries to grab Shriya's arm to stop her from running into the water, but she's already stomping into the surf and leaping into an incoming wave.

"Sharks will come!" he warns as he scans the beach. All the pirates are dead, so he uses scope of the rifle to keep a look out for shark fins.

Something splashes up behind Good Boy, and Shriya swims past with powerful strokes that he can't match. The light from the burning barge debris illuminates the water, but it only helps him to see when a wave rolls under him and lifts him high enough for a view. Every few paddles, his paws slap dead fish and parts of the barge and the Speedwell.

A surviving person screams and splashes somewhere off to his side, but Good Boy doesn't recognize the voice and he doesn't care. He continues to follow in Shriya's wake, but she is too fast. Eyes almost useless and too slow, he concentrates everything on his nose in the hope of finding the faint hint of Calypso under all the horror.

Shriya stops swimming not far away and yells for Calypso. Hoping to hear her alert call and hearing nothing but Shriya and Juan Manuel's muffled call from the distant shore, Good Boy starts to panic.

Think, stupid!

170

Eyes closed and pressing down the fear, he points his nose all around.

There's *something*!

A wave raises Good Boy up and a mat of seaweed floats just ahead of his snout. Paddling after it, the seaweed smells like land trees—Calypso floating on her belly! Good Boy's, insistent, rapid-fire barks call Shriya immediately over to him. Shriya rolls Calypso over. She is still, but strangely intact.

Shriya places Calypso's body on her back with her limp arms draping over her shoulders and tucked through the straps of her bra, then swims as fast as she can back to shore. Good Boy quickly falls behind, resigning to his faith in the people and using what's left of his waning strength to get himself back.

As Shriya reaches the edge of the beach, she drops to all fours and crawls her exhausted body out of reach of the waves, Juan Manuel and Zonda circle around as Shriya gently retrieves Calypso from the straps on her back and lays her still form on the sand. Miguel stands over, shining a light so she can see, watching her pump the little sloth's chest.

"I can't believe it! How did you find her?" he asks with tears falling out of his eyes.

"Good Boy," Shriya says absently, still pumping.

Panting and huffing, Good Boy drags himself over, collapsing into a continuous whimper at Calypso's unmoving side.

Miguel puts a gentle hand on Shriya's shoulder. "I don't think there's anything we can do," he says.

Shriya ignores him and does her best to open Calypso's airway and give her a breath. She pushes on Calypso's chest again and water spits out of her mouth. Another breath, some more compressions and more water comes coughing out.

Calypso opens her eyes to see grainy, flickering beings floating around her. Everything is peaceful and quiet. A dog barks. It sounds far away, but then Good Boy's face looms in front of her. Whimpering, he licks her arms and face and she can only lay there and take it. Shriya is crying over her and Juan

Manuel leaps and dances behind them, calling out triumphantly. Zonda quietly stands off next to the body of Rico. Closing her eyes, Calypso realizes that the bad people must be dead. She hopes Good Boy was able to get Pablo's killer so that maybe he can forgive himself. Like a vapor forming into a thick cloud, her hearing continues to return. Some kind of music plays in the background.

"Is she going to be OK?" Miguel asks.

"I think so," Shriya says, wiping just about every kind of salt water from her face.

"How did you know it was her that crashed the boat?"

"Who else? They must have found the boat somehow and took it back from the pirates."

"I still don't understand how you knew she wasn't killed in the explosion."

"I didn't, but Juan Manuel saw her fall out of the boat."

Miguel shakes his head with an incredulous smile. "How do you know that?"

"I don't know. I just . . . knew." Shriya pauses for a beat, then laughs, recognizing Kenny Loggins' *I'm Alright* coming from the remains of the old Toyota.

"The car stereo is playing the perfect song!" she says. "I can't believe it still works."

"The indicator, too," Miguel observes as the intermittent flashes of the tail light indicator partly lights up the cliff face. "But I wouldn't count on it getting us back home.

"That's OK, I don't think a humble Corolla could ask for a more noble death than squashing some pirates."

"They must have done that, too, these animals! How did they know? How did they know how?"

"They must be watching us far more than we think." Shriya smiles at Juan Manuel dancing. Good Boy, too, watches with an exhausted smile.

Calypso coughs out more water and takes a deep, clearing breath. A little more comes out as she exhales and the feeling in her body starts to return. She's cold, but happy—she did it just like the man did on the magic window tele thing—jumping out of the speeding boat at the last possible moment. Her—a sloth!

Deep breath. Ooh, clear lungs! She coughs up a little more water—*almost* clear lungs. Closing her eyes, surrounded by her friends, Calypso takes another deep breath. All her friends are safe. The sand feels so soft under her head. I love you, beach! She inhales and exhales quietly, and thinks of how wonderful it is to be able to breathe. The people whisper and it's tough to hear them over a strange humming sound. No matter, she has gained enough strength in her arms to move them. Sort of—she lifts them about as high as her chest and they drop back down. Shriya understands and picks her up.

"There must be no way Rondo could have survived," Miguel says, handing Shriya a towel he had found to wrap Calypso in.

Cozy and snug, it smells like people and blood, but Calypso is happy to have it.

"Not unless the pirates lied about him being on the barge, though I don't know where else he'd be," Shriya says sadly. "I heard someone out there on the water calling for help, but it wasn't him."

Miguel pauses to listen for a voice in the water, but doesn't hear anything.

"And if they lied about that, it's probably because they already killed him. Unless he's on the sailboat, but it hasn't moved, so I don't think anyone's on board."

Miguel looks out over the water. Debris and waves reflect the light from the burning remains of the barge. Nothing else moves but the water, same as always, unbothered by fleeting drama.

"I'm sorry," he says softly. "I know he was your friend and even though he didn't like me, I am sad that he's dead."

"He was a good guy," Shriya says, looking out over the water, "he just rubbed people the wrong way because he had to prove too hard to himself that he was better."

"Better than what?"

"Whatever ghosts he had in his mind, I guess."

"That sounds more like demons," Miguel says quietly, stepping towards the water with the rifle scope, scanning the shadows between the dying flames of the burning debris field. "I can't see anyone. Can't hear well, either—my ears are ringing from the explosion."

"Do they hurt?"

"What?"

"Your ears—do they hurt?"

"A little. I don't think they got blown out."

"Did you have your mouth open when the explosion went off?" Shriya asks.

"I don't remember."

"I remember because I was yelling. It's supposed to help equalize the pressure in your head so the high pressure of the blast, followed by the low pressure of its wake doesn't blow your eardrums. Supposed to. I think you're also supposed to cover your ears, but neither of us obviously did that."

Some of the goats tentatively return to the beach to inspect the bodies of the dead men and their herd mates. Juan Manuel walks respectfully over to them.

"It's very dark," Miguel says. "I think we should head up and spend the night at the shepherd's house. Hopefully, the goats will follow us up. In the morning, I'll come back down and bury these poor dead ones. Never in my life would I think I would see the things I've seen. I'm glad you were here to see it, too. Otherwise, nobody would believe it—not even me!"

"They are all absolutely unbelievable and I would die for any one of them," Shriya says, petting Calypso, who is nodding off to sleep in her towel.

Miguel hands Shriya another towel salvaged from the car to dry off with and her clothes that he had collected from the beach. "My eyes will hate me for this, but you look like you're getting cold. At least there don't seem to be any mosquitos. Must be the wind and the smoke."

Shriya smiles and kisses Miguel on the cheek, handing over Calypso so she can get the water and sand off herself before putting her clothes back on.

Once Shriya is dressed, Miguel hands Calypso back to her. "Keep her warm, I'll empty the guns I can find and take a couple of them back with us just in case."

-----------------------|||-------/o) _ (o\-------|||------------------------

Miguel ushers what he hopes are the last of the goats into the pen at the shepherd's house and looks over to the shed where they moved Enrique's body, hoping it doesn't attract predators. He considers leaving the door unlocked so that anything that might come can get at the body instead of turning its attention on the goats. Looking at the two attack dogs and the rifle in his hand that he plans to try to sleep next to, Miguel figures they can probably make it through the night.

"I'll stay with the goats to make sure they feel safe," Zonda says to Good Boy.

"I'll stay out here, too, then."

"No, go inside with Calypso and Shriya. If anything happens, you'll hear me."

"Are you sure?" Good Boy asks. "You're welcome inside, you know."

"That's OK. I'm sure these brave goats will feel safer with me watching out. They can use whatever rest they can get."

"They have Juan Manuel."

Zonda looks to Juan Manuel, who is keeping an eye over the fence facing the fort. "I know," she says, "but he'll need some sleep, too."

"He's not going to sleep," Good Boy says.

"An extra pair of ears, nose, and eyes, then."

"And teeth."

"I hope not!"

Good Boy looks away for a moment, wondering if he should say what he wants to say before returning to her. "I'm sorry about what happened to that man."

"Not too sorry, though," Zonda says, not looking at him.

"I'm sorry for *you*, not him."

"OK, I can accept that. He had bad friends."

"I don't know what you call such people, but those weren't friends," Good Boy says. "Calypso, Juan Manuel, and Shriya are friends. Eh, even Miguel."

"I don't know what you call what you all are, but that's something more than friends."

He smiles and they look at each other for a moment. "Good night," he says to her. "I'm right inside if you need me."

Miguel pats him on the shoulder. "You coming in?" he asks.

Zonda steps back into the pen.

"Come on, girl!" Miguel slaps his leg for Zonda to follow, but she sits. "Fine, I'm too tired to argue with a dog that can eat my face." He latches and secures the gate and Good Boy follows him back to the house.

Miguel closes the door of the shepherd's house and lets out a tired breath. The air is heavy with the weight of a dead man's memories. A teapot sitting on the stove calls out to Miguel. Something stronger would be better, but he'll take it. He becomes aware of the shower going in the bathroom and knocks on the door to see if Shriya wants some tea.

"Come in."

He opens the door and Shriya's hand and Calypso's head stick out from around the curtain. "You're showering with Calypso?" he laughs.

Shriya pulls back the curtain so she can look at him. "I want to get all the sand and whatever else off her and to warm her up. Plus, I figured I could take a better look at her and make sure she isn't injured."

"How is she?" Miguel asks.

"She seems fine, somehow. She seems to like the hot water. I'd ask you to join, but," she looks down at Calypso hanging from her shoulders.

"That's OK. I'm so tired I think I'll just sit in the bottom for a bit."

"You might not want to do that when you see the tub," Shriya grins. "Housekeeping wasn't a high priority for Enrique."

"Says the messiest woman I know!"

"Hey, I'm *messy*, not dirty!" Shriya protests, closing the curtain. "I'm almost done, so let me finish up while there's still enough hot water left for you."

"Speaking of hot water, I was checking to see if you want some tea. The water you put on is ready."

"Yes! Thank you."

Shriya gently pets a mostly dry Calypso, who is resting on top of Good Boy. He is laying at her feet, alongside the kitchen chair where she sits down with a sigh next to a freshly clean Miguel, who smiles and laughs.

"What's funny?" she asks.

"Those clothes—they don't fit at all."

She looks down. "Yeah, you're lucky Enrique was about your size. I guess his wife was really short."

"You might want to keep them with the blood stains and tears on yours."

She glances toward the bathroom where their clothes are tumbling in the washer. "We'll see how well it takes the blood out, but yeah, I *might* be able to save the pants. Where's Zonda?"

"She's keeping watch over the goats."

Shriya goes to stand, then settles back down as Miguel motions for her to sit. "You trust her?"

"She's a shepherd—it's instinct—whatever that is. I thought I knew." He shrugs. "I didn't see the least aggressiveness and there are a lot of goats out there who are ready to fight. They'll be fine."

"I hope so," Shriya says.

"What about you?"

"I hope so. Are *you* OK?"

"I don't think I'll know for a few days," Miguel says. "Calypso seems fine."

"Like nothing happened. She only nearly drowned after stealing a boat that she used to charge a machine gun before jumping out of it at speed, leaving it to crash into a barge that then exploded. So, you know, it's just another day for one of the world's slowest and most docile animals!" Shriya is quiet for a moment, gazing with admiration and affection at Calypso's sleeping form.

"I can't imagine how she would even think to do that." She looks at Miguel. "And there were fish floating all around out there that were killed by the explosion, yet here she still is. It's like they're some kind of immortal guardian angels."

"You becoming religious?" Miguel says.

"No, but when you see so many things that can't be explained rationally, it makes you reconsider what you think you know."

"I hope I don't break any new-found faith," Miguel says, "but it's the swimming bladders."

"What do you mean?"

"The fish. I had an uncle who fished with explosives. The shockwave in the water goes through the flesh of the fish OK, and they would probably be able to survive, but their swim bladders are filled with air. The bladders rupture from the pressure and they die. Sloths don't have swim bladders." He, too, gazes at Calypso. "Could be the shockwave forced the air out of her lungs, though. Good thing it didn't blow out her lungs."

Shriya smiles at him. "Pretty smart," she says.

Miguel shrugs. "Once in a while, I know things. For everything working against them, these animals are very tough." He takes a drink and stares at the ripples in the brown water for a moment, then looks up from his tea. "Maybe it was from the television."

"What was?"

"The idea to crash the boat," he says. "After they watched their animal show a few days ago, I put on *The Hand of the Fourth Shadow*."

"The Kung Fu movie?"

"Yeah. You see it?" Miguel asks excitedly.

"No, you know I don't like those movies."

"Ah, you don't know what you're missing!"

"I feel like I've lived a few of those movies and that's enough for me."

"Yeah," Miguel agrees. "The movie's really not that good, but I like it. The second one was better." They both sit in silence until he suddenly continues.

"The movie starts with the guy who eventually becomes the fourth Shadow warrior on the run from the Yakuza. He's trying to get away from them in his car, but the Yakuza block the road, so he rolls up the floor mat and stuffs it behind the brake pedal so that it holds the throttle down and he jumps out of the car just before it crashes into the roadblock and explodes, killing all the Yakuza except for one, as you find out later."

"A lot of movies have scenes like that," Shriya says, unimpressed, and unconvinced.

"Yeah, but Calypso was watching it! I saw her watching it!"

Calypso opens her eyes slightly and looks in Miguel's direction out of annoyance for how loud he's being, then up to Shriya.

"With her vision, she shouldn't be able to make out much of anything, much less comprehend and remember it, but obviously," Shriya argues gently, "they all watch the animal show. I always thought that she was coming in mostly to be with her friends, but maybe she's able to see well enough to understand what's going on."

"I know what I saw," Miguel says, "and we saw her crash the speedboat into the barge. There is no way she could have survived the crash, so she had to have jumped out. Either she had that idea herself or she remembered that scene. I don't know

179

which one is more incredible." He pauses and frowns. "Of course, we saw goats and a dog come up with a plan to attack a beach to rescue us, so what do I know about how smart animals can be?"

Shriya nods to agree, but her eyelids are too heavy to keep up.

"We should try to sleep," Miguel says. "Busy day tomorrow."

She opens her eyes and takes a deep breath. "Mm. I really wish one of us had our phone."

"I'll go diving under the barge tomorrow. Maybe I can find them, put them in some rice for a while, they'll be good as new."

Too tired to laugh, Shriya manages a smile that turns into a yawn. "Did you go through the pockets of the guys on the beach? Maybe one had a phone? Maybe we won't be able to go too far to get a signal."

"The ones on the open sand didn't, but I couldn't check the ones under the car. I'll see if I can get at them tomorrow. Maybe we'll get lucky again." Miguel stands and takes Shriya's arm to help her up, "Come on, we need to sleep."

What is he doing? Calypso wonders in annoyance as her bed wriggles and stirs beneath her. Rising like a boat in a wave, she finds herself off balance and sliding to the floor. Something smells terrible. Opening her eyes, Good Boy's face is not even an extended reach away scarfing down a pile of meat and eggs. Zonda eats from another plate behind him. An unhurried yawn.

"Are we going home?" she asks, sitting up.

"I'm going with Zonda," Good Boy answers.

"Is she going home?"

"I don't know. Miguel is doing something."

Juan Manuel walks in behind them and looks around. Zonda looks at Calypso's belly and says something to Good Boy that Calypso isn't able to pick up as Juan Manuel greets her at the same time and she greets him back.

Good Boy and Zonda also greet Juan Manuel before Good Boy replies to Zonda. "No, she probably has to relieve herself.

Sloths only go about once every . . . paws . . . tail . . . head of new sky fires."

"Are you sure?" Zonda asks doubtfully.

"Yeah, I've known her since I was a pup."

"OK."

"Do you want to go," Good Boy asks Calypso, "or do you want us to put you in the bed with Shriya?"

"Can you bring me to a tree?"

"Of course."

"Then, I'll go with you." Good Boy lays down and she climbs back up on him.

The secret door bookcase is sticking out away from the wall a bit on one side and Juan Manuel notices an odd smell coming from the behind it, so he goes over for a better sniff. Air coming through. He pushes his nose into the curious vent and the bookcase swings out on the opposite side slightly before rotating inward. Excitedly, he turns to his friends, "Check this out!"

"Yeah, we've been down there," Good Boy says.

"What's down there?"

"Smelly stones," Calypso says dismissively.

"That's it?"

"Spiders," Good Boy says.

Juan Manuel snorts. disappointedly, "Let's go."

The sun is rising with a dazzling demonstration of the fullness of its palette, painting the undersides of the cumulonimbus clouds hanging lazily above. From Good Boy's back, Calypso blinks and narrows her eyes at the light. Reflexively, she reaches for her sunglasses before she remembers that they were lost when she dropped out of the boat. Juan Manuel hugs her with his chin over her back and she reaches around to pet the side of his head.

"You should get on my back so Good Boy can run around with Zonda," Juan Manuel says

"OK."

Calypso climbs onto him and the goats run up to them from behind the fence as they pass. "Where are you going?" A large male speaks for the herd.

"The dogs and the man are going to the beach. I'm bringing her to the trees so she can eat," Juan Manuel says.

"You're leaving us alone? What if the people come back?" Another one asks anxiously from the back.

"They're all dead," Juan Manuel says, "But you shouldn't be stuck in there if you don't want to be." He walks over to the gate and flips the latch for it to swing open. The goats hesitate to leave while Juan Manuel, Good Boy, and Zonda go off on a trot to catch up to Miguel, who is riding a dirty, squeaking old bicycle across the grounds of the fort to the beach.

"What you did yesterday was something I wouldn't even expect from people," Juan Manuel says to Calypso.

"I saw a person do it on the tele thing. I didn't believe it would explode like that because I've never seen anything hit something else and do that, but it turned out to be true. He jumped out of a car, but it's the same. Even hitting the water fast feels more like falling from a tree onto ground."

"It does? I never would have known."

"Don't try it."

"I won't. How did you get out in time?"

She thinks for a moment, "A monkey leaps from branch to branch in a blur. We move with care and we survive because care and determination are just as powerful as speed. Even the dead tree pig didn't seem to understand. He told me that I could choose to be just a sloth or to do great things in spite of being one. I chose to do great things *because* I am one. Any sloth could do what I have done, they just don't have the opportunity or a reason."

"Why leave the trees?"

"Exactly. Too many problems down here and I can't fix them all—I'm out of boats to crash."

Juan Manuel laughs before spotting large birds floating on the air current running up the walls of the crescent harbor.

"Are those harpy eagles?" Juan Manuel asks in alarm.

Good Boy stops suddenly and stares hard, but can't tell from the distance. "I don't know, but they're big."

"Death birds," Zonda says. "Nasty creatures, but they only eat the dead."

Juan Manuel snorts at the reminder of the brave dead goats and Zonda takes off in a run, quickly overtaking Miguel to the forest path down to the beach.

"Zonda!" Good Boy yells after her.

"What's happening?" Juan Manuel asks.

"Rico's body is down there," Good Boy says.

"What's a Rico?" Calypso asks.

"The man that was with her. He was killed on the beach by that woodpecker gun. I woke up more times than I can count last night from nightmares of that thing. Those bullets tore right through the car like teeth through thin leaves and blew chunks off the tree on the beach. Don't even think about what it did to the goats." Juan Manuel says.

Good Boy sighs. "It's too early to run like that and she's too fast."

"It's OK, give her some time alone with him," Juan Manuel responds.

"Yeah. Smart."

"That gun is dead," Calypso says.

"Thanks to you," Good Boy says.

"Yes. Those bullets went through the boat, too. Everything was falling." Calypso pauses, then asks, "How did the car get to the beach?"

"We pushed it off the cliff," Good Boy says.

"Squashed some of the bad people with it," Juan Manuel says.

"Wrong place to be. Why were they there?"

"I don't know," Good Boy says, "they chose that spot to sit."

"No, why were all of them here? Why are *we* here? What is this all about?"

"I still don't know," Juan Manuel says.

"I think it has something to do with those stones in that cave under the shepherd's house," Good Boy says. "Those were the same kinds of stone that Pablo had gotten from the water one time."

"Do the stones make the people this way?" Calypso asks.

"Like some plants can make you see what nobody else sees?" Juan Manuel asks.

"Yeah," Calypso blinks, "like that mushroom the ram wanted me to eat."

"I don't know," Juan Manuel says. "Doesn't do that to me."

"The people like them very much," Good Boy says.

"What for?" Calypso asks. "They're just rock. Rock is everywhere!"

"I don't know why they want it, I've only seen them kill each other and a bunch of my friends to get it." Juan Manuel says in disgust.

"Shriya and Miguel found all those stones in the cave and left them there." Good Boy says.

"They came here for Rondo," Juan Manuel reminds him.

"Oh, yeah, Rondo," Calypso nods. "They didn't find him?"

Good Boy and Juan Manuel slow for a moment and share a look.

"No?" Calypso asks again.

"He was on the small land," Good Boy says reluctantly. Juan Manuel frowns in disapproval.

"Oh," Calypso blinks, then the gravity of it dawns on her. "Ohhh. I didn't know that."

"How could you?"

"You feel OK?" Juan Manuel asks.

"Tired. Hungry. Like I fell out of a tree. Three times."

"Why didn't you stay with Shriya?" Good Boy asks.

"So you can bring me to the trees."

"We're almost to the trees. Want me to leave you there or bring you down to the beach?" Juan Manuel asks.

"I've had enough of the beach," Calypso says.

"So have I."

"Are *you* OK?" Good Boy asks Juan Manuel.

"Not really, but I could be worse."

"Then stay with Calypso up here. You don't need to see those brave goats."

"I feel like I should," Juan Manuel says quietly, "since I convinced them to go out there."

"And you told them what could happen. They knew and they fought for the sake of their shepherd and their future and most of them survived. There is almost no way for us to have taken that beach without some of us never leaving it again and that was before we knew there was a woodpecker gun," Good Boy assures him. "Even if I knew there was such a thing and that they had one, I would have figured that they wouldn't have used it on each other! What can you do against such types of creature?"

Juan Manuel lowers his head. "I know all that and I still feel bad."

"That's OK," Good Boy says, "but try to feel bad about the right things—feel angry about those people."

"I don't want to feel angry."

"Better than sad."

"It is?" Juan Manuel asks, doubtfully.

"Of course!"

"Why?"

Good Boy thinks for a bit. "Because you can't do anything with sadness, but you can use anger to . . ." He stops for a moment and stares out over the water. "Maybe it isn't any better," he finally says.

"This tree!" Calypso says, reaching out to the buttressed trunk of a fig tree.

Juan Manuel stops for her to climb off and he shares a long look with Good Boy. "I think I'll stay up here," he says.

Good Boy nods and heads down to the beach. Juan Manuel watches Calypso climb slowly, effortlessly into the foliage. Another day alive and his old friends are all with him. Closing his eyes, Juan Manuel takes in the smells of the ocean and plants and the sound of the wind and the crashing waves. For a few moments, they're the only things that exist in the world, then with a sudden start, he feels like eating again. Conveniently at his hooves are plenty of plants. The crunch of the plants, the scent released while eating, the flutter of a dragonfly hovering nearby. From behind, he can see the other goats starting to make their way around the perimeter of the fort, tentatively eating what grows around the trees. Why would anyone care about rocks?

The chuff of a shovel spearing into sand. Good Boy arrives on the beach to see Miguel digging up sand to cover the bodies of the goats that he has dragged into a shallow pit. Behind Miguel, Good Boy hears the growling hiss of aggravated vultures protesting the disturbance of their meals and arguing with each other over parts of dead pirates that have washed up on the far end of the beach.

Zonda is laying down next to Rico's body, so Good Boy trots over and lays down next to her, putting his head on the back of her neck. A vulture glides in to land on the rear bumper of Shriya's Corolla like a perch. Good Boy listens to the click and scratch of its talons, following with his head as it shifts along the car's width to the side opposite Rico's body.

A flutter and barely a thump, and it hops down to get a bite out of parts of the pirates that stick out from under the car. Good Boy growls at the rude intruder, but the vulture has different standards of courtesy and it gives a guttural hiss in return, intimidatingly spreading its wings as far as it can in the enclosed space before pecking at an arm and pulling. Good Boy barks, but the vulture continues on the arm.

With a sudden burst, Zonda spins out from under Good Boy and lunges at the vulture that now loses its courage and clumsily breaks for the open beach, getting into the air as Zonda leaps for it, grasping tail feathers in her mouth and nearly bringing the bird down before the roots of the feathers release and she lands back in the sand. The vulture flaps for the cliff top across the bay squawking angrily. Good Boy joins up next to her and Zonda spits out the feathers.

"At some point, they're going to come for him, too," Good Boy says.

"I know," Zonda answers. "It's the way of things, but not while I'm here."

"How long are you going to stay?" Good Boy asks.

She turns to look at Miguel standing over a mound of sand, still working to cover the grave trench of the goats. He leans on the shovel, wiping sweat off of his forehead. Miguel notices the dogs staring at him. Not knowing how to take it, he nods.

"Until he's done covering him," Zonda says.

Zonda walks back over to Rico's corpse and sits down beside him. Good Boy follows and stands vigil beside her.

Miguel understands, and goes over to Rico, cautiously jamming the shovel into the beach and looking at Zonda as he lifts some sand to put it over the body. When she doesn't protest, he continues with the grim work until it's finished. Exhausted and sore, he looks toward the climbing sun, then the remaining human bodies, and shakes his head. He suddenly remembers the other car at the end of the trail that he believes was owned by Rico, so, with Zonda watching, he clears off the sand from about where his pants pockets would be and is able to retrieve the keys. Miguel hopes they can take that car into town and get back with the authorities so they can take care of the pirates. That is, whatever the vultures haven't gotten to.

Juan Manuel watches Good Boy and Zonda come up the now-worn path through the trees with Miguel struggling a bit behind them. The dogs sit down next to Juan Manuel and none of them say a word, settling for the petty distraction of watching Miguel, who finally reaches them and picks up the bicycle. Instead of riding back to the shepherd's house, he rides down the access road. None of them feel like following.

"Is he going back to the town?" Juan Manuel asks after many minutes.

"I don't know," Good Boy says.

"He's getting Rico's car," Zonda responds with a yawn.

"How do you know?"

"Saw him get the jingles from Rico."

"Jingles?"

"I don't know what they are," Zonda says, laying her head on her paws. "They're pieces of smelly metal on a ring. People use them to wake the car up."

"Hm, maybe that's why we had so much trouble getting the car off the cliff," Juan Manuel says.

"No," Good Boy says, "we didn't know what we're doing."

"You two did that?"

"We saw an opportunity to maybe kill three of the people holding Shriya and Miguel prisoner," Good Boy tells her.

She pauses for a moment and raises an eyebrow. "Smart thinking."

"Those people weren't friends of yours, were they?" Good Boy asks.

"None of those men were friends except Rico," Zonda says sadly. "Seeing how you all are with each other, I'm thinking maybe he wasn't a friend, either, but still, he was my person."

"I lost my person, too." Good Boy says. "I was supposed to protect him, but he commanded me to get Calypso and run. I did as he said and they killed him."

"Who did?"

"Some of the people down there."

"*Those* people?"

"They wanted the rocks."

"Those rocks!" Zonda says, disgusted. "What do they want with them?"

"No idea. I only just found out that's what this has all been about. It made more sense when I didn't know."

"They must make something with it," Calypso says from halfway up the tree.

188

"What?" Zonda asks.

"I don't know, but look at all the stuff they make," Calypso says, still tired, and straining to communicate so far.

"There's rock all over the place! What's so special about these?" Zonda asks angrily.

"Don't know. I don't need to make things. Everything I need is all around."

They're interrupted by the sound of the goats calling out. Juan Manuel, Good Boy, and Zonda see Shriya running with a hand holding her boonie hat to her head. The goats gather up behind her and follow in her wake.

"Aren't you going to go to them?" Zonda asks Juan Manuel.

He looks to her, then back at the herd. "They might be running this way to stampede me."

"You're a hero," Zonda says to him. "Didn't you notice last night?"

"Not what I feel like."

"I understand, but that's how *they* feel."

"She is the biggest hero of us all," Good Boy says, looking up to Calypso eating leaves and hanging off a tree branch to bask in the sun with her eyes closed. "And she's unbothered by any of it."

"She also wasn't on that beach," Juan Manuel says.

"Good thing for all of us." Good Boy says.

Zonda also looks up at Calypso. "I still don't know how she survived."

"She jumped out before the crash," Good Boy says.

"Yes, but the fire and the noise that knocked everyone down!"

"Sloths are built tough," Juan Manuel says, walking toward the goats and Shriya.

Shriya runs her hand down Juan Manuel's back as she passes in the other direction, then stops to pet the dogs. "Where's Miguel?" she asks Good Boy with irritation. "He was supposed to wake me up. Is he still on the beach?"

189

Good Boy barks and points his nose down the road.

"Did he head down the road? Why would he . . . oh, I bet he found the keys to that off-roader. Good idea." Shriya heads down the road and after about ten minutes, hears a metallic rattling ahead. Around a bend is Miguel, pushing and leaning on the old bicycle, sweating and breathing hard. She jogs down and takes the bike. "I can take it the rest of the way for you," she says to him.

He's about to protest, but releases the bike and nods, wiping sweat off his face, and bending over with his hands on his thighs for a moment.

"Are you OK?" Shriya asks.

"Yeah, I'm fine," he says after a moment. "Tired and hot. Gave up riding. Had to push. Seemed like a good plan when I only had to ride *down* the hill."

"Rest for a minute." She motions over to some shade and Miguel steps over and sits with his back against a tree.

"Why didn't you wake me up?" Shriya asks, sitting down beside him, leaving the bike leaning on a tree.

"You didn't fall asleep until late, so I let you sleep in," Miguel says. "It's OK, I got the goats buried."

"Were you checking to see if Rico's truck was still there?"

Miguel nods. "I got the keys from his pocket."

"Was it not there?"

"It was, but someone slashed the tires."

"So, there's got to be at least one more of them out there," Shriya says.

"I can't walk all the way back to town," Miguel groans.

"I could ride the bike there. It will take a while, but with our cellphones gone, what choice do we have?"

Miguel takes a drink from his water bottle. "Those guys . . . whoever slashed the tires . . . I think they were the ones Calypso stole the boat from."

"How do you know?"

He points down the road. "There's a road—more of a path—not far past where we were parked. At the end of it is part of a temporary dock. It looks like someone started to take it apart before giving up and fleeing. There are tire tracks from a truck with dual tires and the vegetation is broken along the sides as if something wide had gone down there. I think they couldn't get the truck up here, so they got as close as they could and used the boat to load the explosives they needed to blow the rock when the animals stole it."

"I wonder how they were able to outsmart them," Shriya says. "I would have loved to have seen that."

"Those guys must have heard the blast when the barge blew up and I bet they ran and maybe they slashed the tires on their way out."

"Why would they do that?" Shriya asks.

"I don't know, but who else? I don't think Calypso could swing a knife that hard."

Shriya laughs. "Probably not."

"I wonder why they used the speedboat and not the utility boat to load the explosives."

"Maybe the explosives were more protected in the enclosed boat? They were using the other boat as a shuttle and it would be easier to get people in and out of that than the speedboat." He shrugs disinterestedly, too exhausted to care.

"OK, let's get back to the shepherd's house." Shriya rises to her feet and helps him to stand, then takes the bike to walk it back. "Hey, did you happen to notice if that utility boat was still in good shape?" she asks.

"I should have thought of that!" Miguel says, running his hands through his damp hair and flinging the sweat off his hands. "I didn't look at it, but it was pulled up on the beach at the time of the explosion. Unless some really heavy debris crashed into it, I think it should be OK."

```
-----\o`    `o/---------|||--/o) _ (o\--|||---------  ~`\   /`~  ----
      \      /                                        (       )
       \    /                                          \_/
        \  /
         \/
```

"I don't think I can drive that boat. It has the spinning thing like the big boat on the small land with the weird sheep," Calypso says from Good Boy's back, observing the people inspecting the utility boat on the crescent beach. Shriya rubs her hand over the back of the outboard motor and curses before taking the cover off of it. "What is she doing?"

"You would know better than I would," Good Boy says.

"I only drive them, I don't know what makes them work. Bring me closer. That doesn't look like an animal lives in there."

They approach the motor as Shriya crouches down and swears at it.

"An animal?" Good Boy asks.

"Yeah, the animal that makes it move." Calypso hooks her claws over the lip of the bottom of the motor case and pulls herself up to look at what Shriya is upset about. It smells terrible.

Shriya smiles and pats Calypso's head gently, "That's the motor that makes it go."

Calypso taps the powerhead with her claws and sniffs the oil. "Not an animal," she tells Good Boy.

"What, did you expect to see living under there?"

"I don't know, a whole different kind of animal I never saw before, but it's only another thing the people made."

"Imagine the life of such an animal!" Good Boy says.

"You and I would think it's terrible, but maybe it would be an animal that liked living like that."

"What animal would like that?" Good Boy scoffs.

"I don't know, that's why I wanted to see it!"

"How bad is it?" Miguel asks Shriya from the cockpit, where he is cleaning out debris and looking for damage.

Shriya taps a finger near a hole through the side of the engine and Calypso looks to see leaking, puddled oil, but Shriya looks up at Miguel instead of the oil.

"It's dead. Shrapnel or a bullet or something went through it," she says.

"Dammit," Miguel curses, shaking his head. "Well, at least the hull looks OK. There are some oars in here, but it's going to take forever to paddle this thing."

Calypso settles back down on Good Boy. "It's dead. Bullet."

"I heard."

"It has strange blood." Calypso says, looking up and down the beach. "It must have been really scary here. I could see the lightning flash from where I was on the boat and I knew I had to do something. Now that I see all the buried goats and the parts of dead people, it must have been even worse than I imagined."

"None of us will ever forget it," Good Boy says, solemnly, "and nobody will ever forget what you did."

"What else could I do?"

"Stay where we told you to stay," Good Boy grunts.

"No. Couldn't do that."

"That's why you're the greatest warrior of us all."

She laughs in her silent way and Good Boy turns around to call out to Zonda who is sitting by Miguel. "Zonda, who is the greatest warrior here?" he asks.

"Calypso."

"See?"

"That's ridiculous," Calypso says, blinking. "I can't fight."

"What do you call what you did?"

"Driving a boat badly." She replies, looking around again. "Not supposed to run into things."

"That's fighting!" Good Boy barks. "How is that different than people using guns? There are all kinds of ways to fight."

Calypso decides to drop it as they're never going to agree.

Shriya leans over and pushes down on the transom to pull her feet free of the sand that the waves have closed around her ankles, and replaces the cover. She steps onto the dry sand and looks around at the debris, but there's nothing very useful.

"There are oars?" she asks Miguel.

"Yeah. No oar locks, though. No way we can row all the way back."

"We only need to get to the sailboat."

"That's a pretty big boat," Miguel says. "You know how to sail that? Cuz I won't be any help."

"We'll find out. If I need your help, I can tell you what to do. It's still there, so I'd say it's safe to assume there's nobody on board." Shriya looks at the boat, then back to Miguel. "It didn't sink and it's floating upright, so that's a good sign that any holes in the hull are manageable, and the sails weren't up to get shredded, so that should be no problem. Even if it is, there's a motor."

Miguel stretches his back. "I'm wondering if I should gather the goats up and put them back. If we leave them out, they'll probably wander around and they might get taken by predators. If we put them in the pen, it might be even easier for the predators and they could starve if it takes too long. I vote to leave them out. I don't know if Enrique had any relatives who want the goats, but I hope they let me take them. My cousin and I could expand our business."

"I'll go with your judgement on that," she nods, then scans the debris-strewn beach. "This is going to be a fun one to explain to the authorities," Shriya say. "We obviously can't tell them what happened with the barge. We should tell them that it blew up and we don't know why."

"As long as we tell them where the treasure is, I'm sure they won't care," Miguel says. "Think they'll give us a reward?"

"It would be nice, but what about that curse?"

"The reward would be something different, not a piece of the treasure. At least, I hope so. I'm not an expert on how curses work."

Juan Manuel comes onto the beach with a couple of goats and they survey the long mound of sand that covers their fallen herd mates. One of them climbs on top and bellows out a mournful cry. The rest of the goats cry in unison.

Miguel sees Shriya's eyes tear up and he puts his arm around her. "Goats have souls."

"That I believe. It's people that I'm not sure about," Shriya says, wiping her eyes.

"You and I, maybe. Not those men on the barge. Do you want me to keep Charleston here while you get our stuff or do you want me to get it?"

"Leave it."

"What about the treasure crate I set aside?"

"That was in case we needed to use it to negotiate for Rondo or convince the authorities to come back with us quickly if we escaped. I don't think we need it now."

"Yeah. Sorry about him again."

"Thank you," she nods, looking over at the animals. "I'm glad that the rest of us are alive."

"I thought whatever makes it go is dead," Calypso says to Good Boy as they all step on board the utility boat. She watches curiously as Miguel and Shriya each take a side of the boat and row them away from the beach. "Smart," Calypso nods, "using sticks to make the boat move."

"Slow," Good Boy responds.

"There's nothing wrong with slow," Zonda says, looking at Calypso.

Calypso turns her head to both of them with blinks of impatience. "It is when we want to get home."

Zonda laughs.

"Your home could be any tree," Juan Manuel says.

"It could be if I didn't want to be near all of you," Calypso responds.

"We're not taking this all the way back!" Good Boy assures her. "They're only using this to get to the other boat," Good Boy says.

"What other boat?"

"The big one out there with the tree growing out of it."

Calypso leans her head to the harbor outlet and partly closes her eyes to block some of the bright sunlight, yet she can still only barely make out something floating toward the opening. "It's a tree boat?" she asks.

"I don't know what it's called," Good Boy says. "It's a boat with what looks like a tree coming out of it."

"Like on the tele thing," Calypso says with relief and some curiosity.

A few goats bleat from shore and Juan Manuel bleats back to assure them he will see them again.

Calypso scratches Good Boy behind the ears. "Did you get the bad man who killed Pablo?"

"No," Good Boy cocks his head at an angle to look at her. "He was on the small land you crashed into."

"Then, the boat killed him," Calypso says.

"Good."

"You're not disappointed?"

"Why would I be?" Good Boy asks.

"Because you didn't get him."

"Pablo was just as important to you." Good Boy watches the tree boat get closer. Though the incoming waves are not helping, the people press on, hot and tired, stroking harder against the tide. "I'm done thinking about the dead," Good Boy says quietly.

"So you were right."

"About what?"

"That person who killed Pablo being dead makes you feel better," Calypso tells him.

"No, you were right," Good Boy says. "I almost lost all my friends for revenge on someone who will always be dead."

"I thought we did this to save Shriya and Miguel."

"It was both."

Calypso scratches between the claws of her other hand. "And we *did* both. Stop being mad at yourself."

Zonda laughs and Good Boy puts his head on the floor of the boat and snorts. "At least we didn't do it for rocks."

"What were you going to tell us about the sloth formerly known as Drunk Monkey?" Juan Manuel asks Calypso.

Calypso taps Good Boy on the head to get his attention and looks at each of them, "His new name is *dad*. I have a baby growing in me."

"What?!" Juan Manuel bleats in joy and Shriya and Miguel pause their rowing to look back and laugh at the comical outburst. Good Boy barks in happiness and licks Calypso until she pushes him away.

Zonda smiles at Good Boy, "I told you! You said she just needed to relieve herself."

Calypso blinks disappointment, but Good Boy doesn't notice.

"What do you think happened?" Miguel asks Shriya, returning to paddling.

Shriya smiles, shaking her head in confusion, "I have no idea, but they definitely have some way of communicating that we don't understand."

Good Enough for You, It's Good Enough for Me

The shoreline slides by a short distance away. Shriya adjusts the Oyster 54's sails and the boat accelerates, slicing through the sea and riding gently on the waves with a light heel to starboard. Juan Manuel stands to her left, leaning against the heel with Calypso relaxing on his back and Good Boy to her right and Zonda lying alongside while Miguel sleeps in the cabin.

Calypso watches how the sails respond to the wind, driving them along, leaning them over like a tree in a storm—a tree with no roots. How it works is beyond her, only that adjusting vines behind her allows the sails to best catch the wind while Shriya must also steer the boat with a very large wheel. It's the most fantastic and fascinating thing she's seen that the people can make, and she wonders why all boats aren't like this. Shriya reaches down and pats her head.

"Are you watching how to drive this one?" she asks Calypso.

Calypso gives her a slow blink.

"This kind of boat moves by creating and manipulating pressure differences from the wind. Do you see the sail? It works like a bird's wing . . ."

Mentally exhausted at the thought of it all and everything that has happened the last few days, Calypso closes her eyes to sleep and Shriya smiles and leans over to kiss the top of her head.

The only sound is the rush of the wind and the rhythmic crash of the waves. Shriya makes a fine turn on the helm and adjusts the sails to the new direction. Though her heart still beats fast, her nerves have calmed. The fear, the anger, and the sadness of the last few days has been extracted by the salt air and washed away in the wake of the sailboat, leaving behind a joy she hasn't felt since she sailed as a kid.

Hundreds of years ago, Louis LeFleur cruised this coastline to scavenge off the corpse of a victim of the capricious sea. He probably would have understood what she feels right now—the vast open expanse without road signs or traffic, no need for fuel, no lines but the coast, just freedom at the whims of the ocean and the wind that can drive you home or to adventure or to Davey Jones' locker. Shriya hums a tune that she learned from a few of the old sailors back in the UK. It's a sea shanty made up of verses creatively improvised by the men, often employing humor she didn't understand back then and is probably better off not remembering today, but her own verses start to formulate in her head and she decides to sing them aloud—tired voice be damned, her passengers have undemanding taste.

> "Oh, we'll be allllright if we sail with our friends,
> We'll be allllright if we sail with our friends,
> We'll be allllright if we sail with our friends,
> And we'll all hang on behind.

The wind shifts slightly. Without stopping her song, she tightens the jib a little until the sail telltale ribbons tell their tale of ideal air flow.

> And we'll roll the old chariot along!
> We'll roll the old chariot along!
> We'll roll the old chariot along!
> And we'll all hang on behind!
>
> Oh, some lost Spanish treasure wouldn't do us any harm,
> Oh, some lost Spanish treasure wouldn't do us any harm,
> Oh, some lost Spanish treasure wouldn't do us any harm,
> And we'll all hang on behind.
>
> And we'll roll the old chariot along!" Good Boy howls

along.
> "We'll roll the old chariot along!" Zonda howls with him.

"We'll roll the old chariot along!" Juan Manuel joins in with an extended bleat.

"And we'll all hang on behind!"

Smiling, she pauses for a moment to contain her laughter before being able to continue.

We'll be all right after a good month of sleep,
We'll be all right after a good month of sleep,
We'll be all right after a good month of sleep,
And we'll all hang on behind

And we'll roll the old chariot along!
We'll roll the old chariot along!
We'll roll the old chariot along!
And we'll all hang on behind!"

Calypso blinks awake and shakes her head slowly at all the noise. Miguel comes up from the cabin waving his arms.

"Sorry, was I singing *that* loud?" Shriya says.

"No, but I would like it if you stopped."

"Oh, come on, it's a sea shanty!"

Miguel steps back down and heaves a dark blue duffel bag onto the deck, then comes back up and brings the bag over, lifting with two hands to plop it down on the table in front of the helm.

"Look what I found," he says, unzipping the bag to reveal a pile of paper.

"Is that all money?!" Shriya asks.

"US dollars. Hundreds."

"There must be a million dollars in there—more, even!"

"I didn't count it," Miguel says, zipping the bag back up, "but it's a lot. I checked the serial numbers like in the movies and they are not sequential. They also have the security bands. I am pretty sure they are real. We won't even have to touch the cursed treasure and we don't need a reward!"

"You're OK with this?"

"This isn't part of the curse!"

"It still has blood on it," Shriya mutters.

"All money has blood on it. You don't want your half?"

"Well," Shriya says reluctantly, "I do owe Calypso a new boat."

"And you should keep this one for yourself."

"I don't think it works that way," Shriya laughs. "Besides, it would probably take that whole bag to cover the upkeep for a year! Are you still tired?"

"Of course," Miguel says, "but I'm too excited to sleep any longer."

"Hang out, then. Enjoy the hours before we get to a big enough town to get help."

Speedwell Atalanta

"This is John Speedwell," a voice answers a call from Shriya. "How can I help you?"

"Hello, my name is Shriya Deshpande," she says into a burner phone from her kitchen table, "and I'm looking to order a boat. Are you the owner of Speedwell boats?"

"Yes."

"Do you always take orders from potential customers yourself?"

"It's a small company."

"So, your name is actually *Speedwell*," Shriya says.

"Sort of. It's a translation from the original Polish. Nobody wanted to hire my grandfather with an unpronounceable name during the Great Depression, so it got changed. At least that's how he told it. I think some jerks didn't want to hire Poles, but he thought better of people than I do."

"And you build speedboats now?" Shriya says with a laugh. "How deterministic! You're like a dentist named Fang."

"Or something. A speedwell is a flower."

"Of course—the logo! How unmacho for an American!"

"Yeah, Guns McShootemall, was already taken."

"I'm sorry," Shriya says, "my sense of humor can be abrasive."

"I use mine to sand the boats fair."

"I just meant the joke about the United States."

"Eh, I consider myself a New Englander living under occupation. Reception told me you're interested in a custom order?"

"Well, more of a duplicate, really."

"Swell. Was it a kit or built by us?"

"I'm not sure," Shriya says, clicking a pen open and closed a few times.

"Well, we have full records of our builds, including upholstery swatches, paint chips, wood veneers, whatever. Do you have a hull number?"

"No" Shriya sighs, "I can get that, but I don't have the paperwork on me right now."

"That's OK. If the boat has a name registered with us, I can look it up."

"I didn't see a name. The boat happened to come into my possession through Pablo Rios. I think he's the original owner? He's from—"

"Pablo!" John says happily. "Yeah, he's a character. That was an in-house build . . . dark blue with a red stripe, I think."

"That's the one."

"How's Pablo?"

"He's no longer with us."

John is silent for a moment. "You have my sincere condolences. With the unique things about that boat, I got to know Pablo pretty well. He was one of my favorite customers. What happened?"

"He was murdered," Shriya says. "Shot to death."

John takes another moment before responding. "There are no words for this kind of thing, so I won't cough up any cliché platitudes, but I am truly sorry."

"Thank you," Shriya says. "I didn't know him, I just ended up with his boat. Long story, but his sister sold it to me."

"Ah, OK. Well, I have the plans up on the computer now," John tells her. "Are you sure you want the exact same thing?"

"I'd like it in emerald green, but it has to have all the weird airplane stuff—the controls, sliding canopy, and whatever else," Shriya says. "Oh, could you make the top of the canopy painted like the other ones I've seen online? I don't know what Pablo was thinking with the clear top, but it gets *hot* under there!"

"I asked him, as we paint them even in New England, but he told me it was for night use."

"Ah, of course, right—that explains the concealed night vision setup."

"You like that?" John asks. "The flip up bow mount and remote operation was my design after Pablo said he needed to maneuver around mangroves in low light conditions. The rest of the stuff you mentioned are normal options. I have my own Atalanta set up with the stick and sliding canopy. Most of our customers want more traditional steering wheels, but I'd say close to a third of the builds we do have the control stick option. I was really asking in regards to the unique hull."

"It looked just like the other ones to me."

"They look the same," John says, "but yours uses an experimental composite cloth with extra flotation foam under an extended sole. It's kind of a B4 plus grade armor. There's also a beefed up transom for the larger engine."

"Ha!" Shriya exclaims, banging the table with her fist. Now it makes sense that none of the previous bullets she found when she patched the hull had gone through. "Of course! I don't know what a B4 plus is, but I take it that stops a machine gun?"

"Hm, well, a *sub*machine gun that uses pistol rounds. It's good past .44 Magnum."

"What about one of those machine guns with the stand that feeds bullets from a belt?"

"No . . . well, *probably* not. Maybe with enough distance or at the right angle and with some luck, the hull could take some hits from say, an M60, but I wouldn't bet my life on it. The glass definitely wouldn't take it."

"How was it experimental?"

"It's a prototype," John tells her. "We used the composite as an inner layer since it wasn't quite up to the task for external use. Your new hull would be the same as I can't get a hold of the newer version of the composite. Pablo and I talked about the fighter plane aesthetic and got into talking about armor and I knew this guy who was developing this composite and Pablo agreed to front a large portion of the development costs to incorporate it into a boat. I didn't ask him what it was needed for, but I imagine there's a connection to why he's no longer with us?"

"I don't know why he was killed," Shriya says, "but I'd guess it had something to do with smuggling." The sound of

Calypso's door shutting comes from the living room. Good Boy and Zonda's nails click along the floor as they trot past the open kitchen doorway to greet her.

"Well," John continues, "if you don't need the bullet-resistant hull, it will save you a lot of money and time, plus you can get by with a smaller engine. If you do want the *extra durability*, it's not my business what your business is, though I am a bit curious what someone would use such a small boat for besides maybe as an armored yacht tender."

"I'm a paleontologist."

"Really?"

"Yes."

"That's awesome! Extinct or not, I like animals better than us." John says, "I do have to disclose that nobody has tested the hull against mosasaur teeth in case there are some still hanging out somewhere."

"No mosasaurs. I study prehistoric megafauna that came after the K-Pg extinction. Giant ground sloths are a specialty of mine."

"Those were the ones the size of bears?"

"Some of them were the size of elephants."

"Interesting." John says. "I have something new to research tonight. Anyway, if you don't want the experimental material, we can build it with the standard hull and you'll still have the other one if you want to chase looters or something."

"That boat's gone" Shriya says, "so I'm looking for a new one to replace it."

"Stolen? I can't imagine it sank with so much flotation."

"Well, it blew up, so . . ."

"It blew up?" John exclaims. "Hey, we didn't rig the boat—Pablo had that done locally."

"Uh, no, well, it hit a barge full of pirates, and I'm pretty sure it was loaded with explosives at the time."

"Was it Blackbeard's ghost?" John asks with a laugh. "Even being dead, I hear he can be a tough customer."

"They weren't technically pirates, they were criminals who were trying to steal the treasure from the shipwreck of an old Spanish galleon."

"How was it . . .?" John pauses for a moment, then says, "Wait, is that the thing I saw in the news about an old treasure that was found when authorities were investigating an explosion?"

"Do you like stories?"

"The only things that make us human are art and stories. Probably."

"I promise to tell you the most incredible story you've ever heard if you can do me a favor."

"Sure."

"This is going to sound shady, but can you declare the Speedwell's value as a very depreciated used boat? I'll pay the full cost."

"Trying to get around import duty?"

"Not quite. You'll understand if you hear the story."

"What if I sell you my personal boat? Won't be shady that way, cheaper, and no wait to build. Of course, I'll go through it and touch up whatever needs a little work."

"That sounds great, actually," Shriya says, a bit relieved.

"I'll send you pictures and, if you want it repainted or whatever, we can get that done."

Shriya takes a deep breath. "Hey, so I don't know your schedule, but if you can find a way to come down to Costa Rica for the delivery or whenever, I can tell you the story. As a fellow animal lover, I think you'll be amazed. I don't want to say more over the phone."

John nods and looks across his desk at the scribbled phone number on a pad for his potential divorce lawyer and up at a picture of an old blue Subaru Legacy wagon. The silver frame has the name *Duchess* written in a black Art Deco typeface. "Yeah, it's about time I go on another road trip."

"You're going to drive all the way down here?"

"I could use the time to think."

Captain Calypso

With the goat pen having gotten crowded from the arrival of Enrique's goats, Miguel and his cousin are pounding posts into the ground to expand the fence line. Their land maintenance and clearing business now has enough goats to tackle big projects, or several smaller ones at once, and they're expanding to add tree planting and forest restoration on the scrub-cleared land along with the installation of raceways that use ropes to tie broken tree canopies together for arboreal animals to more safely travel to new areas without having to risk electrocution on power lines or face dangerous road crossings and animal attack on the ground.

Calypso rides Good Boy up the road with Zonda alongside, just about the safest sloth in the world. Her baby boy clings to her own back, his tiny face in the air to take in the smells of the low lands. In the tradition of the people, she has named him Pablo. By coincidence or rare breakthrough in telepathic communication with a human, Shriya has taken to calling him the same name.

"Mom, this is the corner we turn, I know it!"

Calypso's heart swells with pride. "Yes, you remember the way, now?"

"Yes, I remember! And I smell the goats, too."

They pass the last trees before turning to the driveway that runs alongside the goat pen and, within moments, the goats crowd the fence to see her and Pablo. Even the old donkey who guards the herd stands above to see, unconcerned by the dogs. All the attention is tiring, but Pablo likes to watch the goats and they get so excited when she shows up that Calypso makes the journey every once in a while. She does rather enjoy seeing the kids jumping around, butting heads, or chasing Juan Manuel while he feigns fear.

Ever since that fight on the beach, Calypso has noticed that when Juan Manuel is alone, he has a bit of the far-off look to him that Good Boy once had, yet when the kids chase him or he sees her, he's the same old Juan Manuel. Good Boy is more laidback now that he has Zonda and Zonda has adjusted to her new family, though none of them could ever be who they were before the horrors and wonders of their adventures.

Calypso imagines it must be more difficult for the social animals. Experiencing things so differently than the rest separates them from their group, making them feel uneasy in a way that must be similar to how she feels when she's out of the trees. Every time she visits, the adult goats tell the kids about the fight on the beach and Calypso's charge of the woodpecker gun in the harbor, but since they can't understand it, they don't seem especially interested and she's happy that Pablo's grasp of Common language is still too weak to understand what they are saying so that she doesn't have to explain. Her son doesn't need the burden of her history. It's enough to learn what it takes to survive in their world and she knows with her friends around, her little one will be as safe as any sloth could be. No smelly rocks, no fast boat, no power over other big monkeys could matter so much.

Stephen Kappotis grew up on the North Shore of Massachusetts and enjoys writing, design, history, zoology, wood working, machines, and making things.

The idea for this series began while working on a compact speedboat design that uses an aircraft-inspired control stick for steering and motor trim while watching videos of rescued sloths opening doors, using a toilet (more or less), and teaching these skills to others. At one point, the image of a sloth operating the boat's simple controls came to him and he began to wonder what her story could be. Being a sloth, she needed a faster way to get around on land, which led to a dog character for her to ride like a horse. Not wanting to simply write anthropomorphized animal characters, he attempted to account for the differences in perspective that would come from the varying lifestyles and senses of the characters while balancing an ability to communicate in a manner needed for the story. Inspired by old myths of capricious gods and flawed heroes overcoming their often humble origins to accomplish great feats and triumph over powerful adversaries, the story soon developed into this series, *The Voyages of Sloth and Good Boy.*